To Elizabeth for her support and patience

To
Marguerite Effel
and to
Jean Effel
Creator of Heaven
And what it contains,
Father of Angels,
Brother of the Fairies,
Patron of Academicians,
- this 'cup of tea'
with my friendship.

P.V.

THE OLD LADIES' TEA PARTY

by
PIERRE VÉRY

Translated from French by
ALAN GRIMES

Francophile Press

Francophile Press

4 Harmer Lane, Cringleford
Norwich, Norfolk NR4 7RT
www.pierrevery.co.uk

ISBN 978-0955243-929

Typeset in 11pt Bembo by Troubador Publishing Ltd, Leicester, UK
www.troubador.co.uk

CONTENTS

ACKNOWLEDGEMENTS

Noël Véry, the son of Pierre Véry, is concerned actively with promoting his late father's work for English-speaking readers. He and his wife have entertained my wife and me on several occasions and his enthusiasm has provided a valuable insight into his late father's approach to writing the 'fairy tales for grown-ups' which have made him a popular author in France.

As with two previous books in this series John W.J.Fletcher, Emeritus Professor in the University of East Anglia, has been kind enough to cast his professional eye on the script with resulting benefit. I am again most grateful.

The cover illustration for the present novel, as for several earlier translations, was carried out by Faye Briony Pearson and I am grateful to her for her skilful and apposite portrayal.

I am particularly grateful to my wife, not only for her support and patience, but especially for her considerable grammatical contributions to the text.

Jeremy Thompson of Troubador Publishing Ltd. has once again been of great assistance in steering me through the complications of self-publishing.

Any translational problems arising from my treatment of the original text can be taken up via:

alanlizgrimes@btinternet.com

*Trustworthy astrology for predicting the future with certainty will
not be discovered so long as the earth is inhabited by men who
have a fear of death.*
A. de THYANE
(Practical treatise of elementary astrology)

*"Thanks to my gifts of Seeing and to my knowledge of the Occult
Sciences, I will reveal your Past to you, explain your Present to
you just as if I had always lived close to you, which really proves to
you that I can reveal your Future ... .
The total cost of my fees for a complete and very detailed
Horoscope is set at 150 francs. As your case is one of the most
interesting that I have had to study, I will make you an offer of a
special price of only fifty francs."*
THE FAKIRS

*Fakirs live on public charity, spending their lives without working,
homeless, and for clothing have only a scrap of material around
their loins.*
Le Petit Larousse

THE OLD LADIES' TEA PARTY

Curled up, on the bedside rug … Dead. He was lying on his left side, nose in his waistcoat, fingers clasped over his stomach. The collar of his coat was soaked in blood. There was a large, brown sticky stain on the rug. Someone had planted a kitchen knife in his neck.

'And to think,' reflected the lawyer, that this started with butterflies! I have been led as far as here by a four-in-hand of butterflies, - like the fairies of earlier times! And then, there has been this number 126! And the number 127! And the pacing up and down of the dwarf! The sessions of the postwoman in front of her wardrobe mirror! And this mute, prattling like a magpie! … '

Ah, chance had set up his little plot very well! His own scheme of course! … .

But we must begin at the beginning … .

CHAPTER 1

THE CODED MESSAGES

'Criquebec is somewhat dead at the moment,' the widow observed.

On the Square, three words were heard ringing out, always the same : 'Blue ... white ... red ... . Blue ... white ... red.'

'Who's that parrot?' the man asked.

'Nothing,' the widow said. 'It's the Bladout's girl. The layabouts who live in the muck!'

She let out a faint sigh.

She was a larger woman than the widow Angat – six feet three inches in height, fifty-four inches around the waist, twenty-three stone in weight.

She put out a finger like a podgy sausage towards the window, moved the curtains very slightly apart and threw a glance on the Square over the top of her pince-nez which trembled at the end of her flabby nose.

The young girls were playing at 'Portraits.' They were mimicking the personalities of the town – Lecorbin the mayor, Andréa Gauric the schoolmistress, the mute Barnaby, the dwarf Couril, the widow Angat, Mr. Jaufre, Médéric Plainchant, Aubin the village policeman. From the walk, the intonation, the official gestures or the mannerisms, they had to guess who.

In the distance the young Bladout was leaning against a chestnut tree. She was wearing a yellow pullover and a spinach-green dress, from which stuck out a good hand's width of scarlet slip. She was devoting herself completely to this game of her own invention which consisted in shouting indefinitely three names of colours. She marked no intervals between the words, so that one got the impression that she spoke only one, without any meaning : 'Bluewhitered … . Bluewhitered.' To cap it all, this little worm had a voice sharp as a thorn.

'And it's only the beginning of August!' The widow Angat groaned.

Until school started again, she would have her eardrum bored into by this sort of piercing incantation!

She let the curtain fall back. In one second she had seen everything that it was possible to see. They have good eyesight in the provinces! – the young Bladout, the girls, the baker's pug emptying his bladder against the central milestone, Francis Couril, the vain dwarf, pacing up and down, his stomach hung with a gold watch, seeing no-one – or giving the impression of not seeing – ignoring greetings when by chance a poor village simpleton doffed his hat, and pondering on who knew what thoughts. Or rather yes, one knew very well what! Nothing good!

She had noticed in Mrs. Gentil's pharmacy the presence of the servant of Maître Figuier the solicitor (what remedy was she buying?), a peasant come by bicycle to Frelasset the butcher's place, and two women in Fernande Vasseur's shop (people she had not been able to recognise). Miss Zélie Beluge, ever the playful one, was laughingly showing to Médéric Plainchant from a distance a baby that she was bouncing on her arm (whose nursling might this be?). On old Jaufre's doorstep the mute Barnaby, in this costume so patched it made him look like Harlequin, was sawing logs and making himself angry. The presbytery chimney was giving off a puff of smoke. A fire in this heat? Surely someone was poorly! Knowing whether it was the priest or his servant?

Besides, even if the widow, strictly speaking, had been unable to identify them, hadn't she at any rate guessed at the

2

profile of an old woman on watch behind each window of each house around the Square, fingers imperceptibly moving the curtains apart.

For the third time she sighed (they sigh a lot in the provinces!)

'One feels unwell! Worse than unwell! Exhausted!' The man agreed.

An odd character, this fellow! Tall, slim, around forty-five, thin mouth, hooked nose, yellow eyes flecked with black, he made one think of a sardonic owl.

His look was disquietingly steady. Even the bland manner in which he lowered his eyelids, surprisingly prominent and which seemed of velvet, offered little comfort!

He was able to maintain at length a fascinating immobility.

He considered the periwinkle blue wallpaper, the ultramarine double curtains, the Prussian blue fabric which was stretched over the armchairs. In a window corner, a small disc of royal blue satinette was pasted to the glass.

Above one of the double doors a radiating globe was painted. In Gothic lettering this name – *Jupiter.* A little lower, an arrow, the astrological sign representing the constellation of Sagittarius.

A small clock sounded four shrill chimes.

'Here is Fernande Vasseur,' the widow announced. She burst out laughing into her hand.

'Fernande Vasseur,' the man asked, 'she's the one who –'

'The one who believes in Numbers – yes! She's going to experiment on you, you'll not avoid it!'

Fernande Vasseur showed her sixtyish years. She was dried up and yellow. She had a prying air and a frightened manner which arose from a scolding, irascible husband.

She did not notice the man, who was standing silently in the half light. The widow raised her enormous weight and moved forward with an elephant's trot.

'Delighted to see you, my good Vasseur!'

'And me too, my good Angat! You are bearing up?'

'My arthritis is giving me trouble. You know that Friday is my adverse day. Saturn is not relenting!'

'Jupiter will see to it, don't worry!' Vasseur replied, in a tone in which the man detected no irony.

The widow smiled sweetly and asked: 'What news?'

'Andréa Gauric lost her action against Gratoulet. That was risky for her! Gratoulet has the deputy in his pocket. I'm very pleased!'

'I thought that Andréa Gauric was among your friends?'

'Of course! I'm furious that she has lost, but am happy to see that my prediction has come true. I had made the calculation by the Key of the Double Zodiac.'

The widow directed a sign of complicity to the man loitering in the shadows – as if to say: 'You understand? She's starting!'

'Andréa Gauric's bizodiacal number is 77,' the visitor continued, very agitated. 'That of Gratoulet, 78. Divide by 9. 77 gives the remainder 5. 78 gives 6. Consult the Chart of numerical Victories, you will note that 6 beats 5. I explained it to poor Gauric; I showed her the Chart; I said to her: "You are wrong to dig your heels in, Andréa! The numbers are against you! Even though you could have the best lawyer in the world … ." But I was preaching in the wilderness! Andréa is a strong character, she uses only her head. And there's the result! Now she's going to appeal to Rouen! Ah well, she will lose again!'

The man gently coughed. Fernande Vasseur jumped.

'A thousand pardons, sir! I didn't notice you in the darkness … . My dear Angat, I didn't know that you had someone; I'm off, I will come back later.'

'Not at all! Not at all!'

The man approached.

'I present Mr. Prosper Lepicq to you.' The man saluted.

'Very honoured,' Fernande Vasseur said. She ran a business on the Square in corsets, suspender belts, girdles, and other hygiene and female beauty commodities. Astutely, she had christened her shop *The Wasp Waist*. A flattering sign, if one reflects that the widow Angat (54 inches around the waist!) and a sprinkling of matronly women of a tonnage almost as impressive made up the core of her clientele!

'Would you believe, Mr. Lepicq,' the widow suggested, 'that my friend Vasseur is capable of divining your profession, your character, and even your future, from nothing but the sight of your name!'

'Impossible! … .'

'Angat exaggerates!' Vasseur simpered for convention's sake. 'Nevertheless, if you'll allow it, I can try … .'

She wrote on a piece of paper the name of Prosper Lepicq, noted down a number for each letter, then added: 'This is the way of the Hand of Fatima. These numbers correspond in mystical interpretation to the letters. I notice that the total gives 592. 592 is your personal number.'

'I find it agreeable,' said Lepicq, amused.

Vasseur pulled a worn booklet from her bag. 'I'm referring to the numerical Chart of Conformities from the hand of Fatima and I'm breaking down your number. 500 signifies *choices, honours, statures.*'

'This is too flattering!' Lepicq spoke modestly.

'Let's see now, 92 … Ah! How odd … .'

'What then?'

'92 foretells *destruction, death, disaster.*'

'That's less cheering!'

Fernande Vasseur pondered. 'I see … . Through ruin and death you reach honours! Conclusion: you must be in the army. Let's say colonel. Did I hit the nail on the head?'

'Not exactly, dear lady! I am a lawyer of Assizes.'

'Ah!' she said, nonplussed. But she recovered quickly.

'Would you say that you act for murderers?'

'Exactly that!'

'Very well! Officer ... . Lawyer ... . The oracle applies itself to both professions! It is in your occupying yourself with people who cause death that you will achieve celebrity status – if it has not already happened!', she added amiably. 'Be indulgent of my ignorance – it's the provinces, isn't it –.'

Meanwhile, on the square the young girls were playing tag. To know who was caught they recited at top speed: '*Am Stram Gram, Femina Godam, Carabim Zigolo, the Capital city at Mother Angot's!*'

This modified version of a mantra, which the man undoubtedly believed adjusted by childhood wisdom, had been brought back from Rouen by a senior girl with a school leaving certificate.

'You've not been in Criquebec long, Mr. Lepicq?' asked Fernande Vasseur, who knew perfectly well that the lawyer had arrived two evenings ago. 'You're planning to remain some time with us?'

'I don't know for sure.'

'I hope we don't owe the pleasure of having you with us to a murder, or to I don't know what ugly business?'

'Rest easy, Madam! I'm on holiday. A piece of luck, for which I'm thankful, led me to Criquebec.'

It was true. A stroke of luck. The greatest stroke of luck.

'I've been captivated by the charm of your very picturesque town ... .'

That was a lie.

But Prosper Lepicq, the famous lawyer-detective, had no wish to reveal to the worshipper of numerals that it was precisely because of two numbers that he had changed his plans, and made up his mind to make a stop in this locality in lower Normandy where his whim had led him.

126 ... . 147 ... .

The possession of two numbers sent to him by chance. Two coded messages ... .

'Numbers,' Fernande Vasseur uttered meaningfully, 'it's frightening when you think about it! If I told you that my husband, in his year, took an average of twelve million steps!'

'Ah, really! Lepicq was taken aback.

'It's very simple! My husband is a postman. By and large, his rounds amount to twenty kilometres. Let's say that outside work, for going here or there, rotating around a billiard table, doing nothing, he still walks his five kilometres. At the end of the year, that gives you nine thousand kilometres! At seventy-five centimetres per step, you have the twelve million I mentioned!'

126 … . 147 … , Lepicq reflected. To appear part of the conversation, he remarked, 'in fifty years, that makes six hundred million steps! That's fantastic!'

The lawyer and the corset dealer were standing completely still. Only the widow was moving a little – just a little! … . Nothing but this gesture, which she made every two minutes – putting out a finger to separate the curtain by a centimetre, for one second.

Although there were no other flowers in the room apart from an armful of honesty, a very faint perfume was wafting. A yellowed photograph was displayed in a frame near the imposing widow, a small, scrawny man, black as a cricket and the owner of an old soldier's moustache – the late Ernest Angat.

A scratching came from the kitchen. The old servant Noémi was scraping the bottom of a bowl in which she planned to make jam. They heard a cry, followed by mutterings, and the servant came into the sitting room. Her right thumb, down the length of which ran a trickle of blood, was stuck comically in the air.

'You've cut yourself, my poor girl! We must put on some fleur de lys'.

'No, no,' Noémi said. 'Nothing like a spider's web. I'm going up to the loft to find one.'

The widow and Vasseur shrugged their shoulders. A spider's web for healing cuts, it was another of Zélie Beluge's recipes! Just what was needed to infect a wound!

7

CHAPTER 2

CRIQUEBEC

Prosper Lepicq, the Parisian lawyer-detective, had had a particularly full winter and Spring. Consequently, this summer he had resolved to treat himself to some holiday.

But a holiday as few people still dream of enjoying them, holidays which make a real rest for the mind; romantic holidays; a pleasant journey on foot.

He had invited his young secretary Jugonde to take part in the trip. A deep affection united the lawyer and the adolescent, fuelled by the memory of numerous risks experienced together. However, the young man had turned down the invitation. Ill at ease, he had ended by admitting that he had fallen madly in love the previous evening! Love at first sight!

'You have gained all my pity, my poor friend!' Lepicq joked. 'During my absence you will be kind enough to call in here, from time to time, to put your nose in the post.'

Then he was gone, quick-footed, along the Avenue des Champs-Elysées, Avenue de la Grand-Armée, Avenue de Neuilly and the Ministry of Defence.

His destination was Le Havre.

In a leather briefcase – a contemporary replica of the old journeyman's bundle – he carried two shirts, two sweaters, two pairs of boxer shorts, a bathing slip, three pairs of socks, six handkerchiefs, pyjamas, a pair of slippers and the complete Essays of Montaigne in one volume, uncut.

★ ★ ★

Very tranquil, he had sauntered on his way along the twists and turns of the Seine towards the Channel, stopping to dive in and make several breast strokes as the fancy took him, moving on scarcely more rapidly than those barges hauled by one-eyed horses.

He met fishermen, swimming enthusiasts, nudists, lovers – no-one but good folk! The idea that there exist throughout the world creatures who kill their fellow men to rob them, or through jealousy, or for any other futile reason, had effectively left his mind! He lunched, had dinner and lodged where he fancied. Idleness governed his timetable, the nature of the scenery his route. He experienced such a feeling of freedom, of escape, that his behaviour ended up by suggesting the idea of illegal vagrancy!

In this way he managed his modest average of twenty-five kilometres per day (hardly as much as postman Vasseur!) without thinking to ask himself how many steps he would make at this rate in a year ... . He did not once open the Montaigne but in the evening, before yawning one last time and closing his owl's eyes for six or seven hours, he took a childish pleasure in fingering the volume to wonder at its thickness!

Then the murderers drifted to the surface. The lawyer reflected that after all they have their merits and that he was really rather ungrateful to them! In killing everyone, they provided his livelihood!

He put the Montaigne down, switched off the light, turned himself onto the right side and gently closed over his yellow eyes the velvet lids round like walnut shells.

★ ★ ★

A week of this routine and our decoder of enigmas had arrived some sixty kilometres from Havre.

Abreast of Caudebec, why does he feel the desire to distance himself from the river? Simply because a hill topped with young oaks tempts him towards it! On the other side of the prominence, the wish to visit the abbey of Saint-Wandrille. But, when he reaches the valley he has already forgotten his intention! Where is he going? He's going to Yvetot! Yvetot? Good idea! Actually, why Yvetot? No reason! Perhaps because of Béranger's song … .

But on the path, a meadow of butterflies presents itself. Seductive, with the apple blossom. Lepicq involves himself in it.

So much the worse for Yvetot!

It was in this way, guided by the butterflies, sensitive to all enticements, wonderfully receptive, that Lepicq arrived at the edge of the basin where the small locality of Criquebec was simmering under the sun.

How four hundred souls had found themselves of a good enough social mix to consent to come setting themselves up on the sides of this chalky crater in order to cook, love, suffer, sleep and dream there, let him who can explain!

Criquebec had only one square. This was the *Square*. Circular, bordered by some twenty dusty chestnut trees, it occupied the bottom of the basin – a base ablaze on days of luminous intensity, and steaming in times of heavy rains.

It was the evening hour when a pleasant drowsiness stiffens the hamstrings and relaxes the thigh muscles. The hour when the prospect of slumping on a cane chair on a café terrace in front of an absinthe, leaning back stretching the legs up to the end of the county, on the lips a slight smile which is inclined not to say great things, but which says exactly what it wishes!

Prosper Lepicq had allowed himself to slip through the crooked alleyways as far as the Square. On the terrace of the café – restaurant, the Pibole Hotel of Commerce and Sports, he was slumped, tilted back. He had been served a very green and pleasant absinthe in which was floating a good lump of ice. He told himself that for the moment at any rate, green was the finest colour which existed! A true proof of the existence of God! And the cane chair was also proof of the existence of God!

'*Am Stram Gram* ...' the young girls were squealing, between a couple of slightly irritated looks at the 'stranger'. Lepicq was telling himself that they were very good and agreeable girls. A dwarf of some forty years was pacing up and down on the Square. He had a rather ill-tempered appearance, he had to behave himself, and he was walking angrily. However, Lepicq told himself that he didn't in the end have to be an unpleasant dwarf! Anyway Criquebec seemed in general a very good little town, whose inhabitants looked well – an appearance pleasant and frank ... . From bliss, the lawyer slipped to the foolish. But he was intelligent enough to understand that from time to time he had to be aware of becoming foolish; it's good for the health!

Erected exactly in the centre of the Square was an amazing rectangular pillar, one and half metres in height and dazzling white. It carried this inscription in black letters:

Criquebec Town
Canton of Caudebec
District of Yvetot
Lower Seine

This ludicrous pillar, an invention of the mayor Mr. Léonce Lecorbin, reminded one of an envelope with the inscription as an address – an address which had omitted only the name of the addressee, whom one readily imagined in the guise of a character of the size of his post – a giant!

'This is a very beautiful pillar!' Lepicq told himself, open to all indulgences. He threw a glance over the façade of the café – restaurant – hotel Pibole and straightaway judged it a very sympathetic and comfortable establishment.

'I'm going to dine very well! And sleep very well!'

In fact he dined very well.

But he was pretty far from knowing that as for sleeping... .

★ ★ ★

The incident happened on the stroke of eleven.

Lepicq's room contained two windows opening on to the Square, one to the south-east and the other to the south-west. Lepicq had put out his light. His braces hung down the length of his legs. His trousers fell over his slippers. Arms crossed, he was enjoying a cigar. On the Square a street lamp was giving out a flame into the soft evening. The houses bordering the Square were immersed in shadows, with the exception of two. The lawyer was easily able to direct his gaze at the one straight ahead where, on the first floor, was standing a pink and podgy sexagenarian.

The man had given himself over to gesticulations designed to attract the attention of another person, also illuminated, in the building opposite. It was enough for the lawyer to move himself over to the west window to observe a slim woman of roughly similar age to the man. On a large sheet of paper, the latter drew an inscription with charcoal. He raised the sheet and went over to an oil lamp, so that the woman was able to decipher it despite the distance. Leaning out, Lepicq managed to read it too. The man had simply written a number: 126.

The woman seemed a victim to some irritation.

In her turn, she bent over a sheet of paper. Lepicq bounded over to his west window and took note of the response – also a number: 147.

Shortly after, the lamp of the woman was blown out – then that of the man.

Amused, Lepicq slipped on his jacket and went downstairs. On the Square, feebly lit by the hissing street lamps, he located the buildings which interested him. A cutlery shop occupied the ground floor of the sexagenarian's house. Over the shop this sign reading: *For the Good Swordsman.* On the glass door, a name in enamelled letters:

Médéric PLAINCHANT
Son of the founder

On the other side of the Square there was also a shop kept by a Miss Zélie Beluge. The sign sent the lawyer into raptures: *For the Wish to Please.*

The window testified effectively to a strong desire to please the small and great. There were there haberdashery items, comics, fashion magazines, paper flowers and doves for end of year wishes and sentimental declarations, fishing tackle, toys, dolls, imitation faeces, imitation pistols with rubber arrows, percussion caps, firecrackers, glass jewellery, marbles, balls, dominos, safety paints, paper flags, packets of collector's stamps, cycle lamps, charming and useless odds and ends, and even a whole assortment of physical and chemical 'jokes and tricks': snowstorm tablets, shivering ribbons, glacial liquid, sparkling handshake ('Madam, I'm shaking your hand with sparks!'), the devil's matchstick, the devil's screw (the most comical), and vanishing paper, and endless string, and amazing rings, not forgetting the 'nose trumpet', also known as Head Cold! Plenty to laugh about and amuse the family!

Lepicq smiled, blowing the smoke of his cigar to the stars.

'What a delightful little town! And what good children the inhabitants!'

It was a clear night.

Before returning to his hotel, the lawyer walked a little. This stroll led him to a large crossroads: the Patte-d'Oie-du-Petit-Roi. There also a light was burning, on the first floor of a dilapidated building. It went out as Lepicq appeared. At the same moment the lawyer saw a silhouette by the Patte-d'Oie. It slid furtively along a wall, and disappeared into an alley. Then there was the noise of running. Lepicq continued his walk and came across another person; it was the mute Barnaby. He was talking to himself, that's to say he was uttering grunts meaningless to anyone but himself. A violent anger was making him gesticulate.

'Delightful little town!' Lepicq repeated. But the tone of voice was changed!

These incidents were enough to put the lawyer-detective into a mood of no longer noticing that after curfew time strange mysteries were unrolling all around Criquebec!

★ ★ ★

The following morning, as he took his café au lait on the terrace of the hotel, he caught sight of Médéric Plainchant. The cutler was sprinkling his pavement before sweeping it. He seemed gloomy. Zélie Beluge showed herself on her doorstep. She had a cheerful air. The cutler quickly opened his right hand wide, then closed it, keeping only the index finger raised.

'Well, well!' Lepicq said to himself. 'The fun of coded messages goes on! Five fingers plus one equals six.'

Zélie Beluge vanished into her shop, reappeared soon after and traced the number 39 on her window with whitewash, which she quickly rubbed out. Leaving his sweeping , Médéric Plainchant shut himself in the cutlery shop.

The lawyer went back into the hall of the hotel Pibole.

'All things considered, I'm not leaving today! I mean to rest here for some days.'

★ ★ ★

14

Again that evening, Lepicq had the satisfaction of seeing the strange signalling repeated. Zélie Beluge opened up the conversation with the number 101. Plainchant responded with 56 and 85. In reply, Zélie sent 20. Plainchant came back with 158, which had the effect of dragging a brief and shrill laugh from Zélie. Then the two lamps went out together.

It was evident that the man and the woman had agreed on a 'code'. Each number corresponded to a phrase decided in advance.

While reflecting, Lepicq reached the Patte-d'Oie-du-Petit Roi where, the day before, a mad rush had followed the dousing of a light. He could not have hoped that the two incident were repeating themselves. Nevertheless, that is what happened!

Promptly, the lawyer turned back, ran the length of the two intersecting alleyways and planted himself in a corner. The lookout of the Patte-d'Oie was arriving – it was the dwarf Francis Couril!

The flat under whose windows he was on watch was occupied by a youngish-looking woman of around forty: Reine Coulemelle, a postal worker.

A short distance away the lawyer saw again the mute Barnaby, gesticulating and vociferous.

Strange little town!

★ ★ ★

The following day, a new coded dialogue:

'Nine,' said Médéric Plainchant
'Sixteen,' answered the jokes and tricks merchant.
'Thirty,' replied the cutler.
'Eighteen,' Zélie Beluge retorted.

CHAPTER 3

WIDOW ANGAT'S DRAWING ROOM

Every day from four until six the widow Angat held court. That's to say she received half a dozen ancient lunatics. Zélie Beluge, whom Lepicq wanted to observe, made up part of the coterie. The lawyer had introduced himself to the widow through the hotel-keeper Pibole.

'These ladies tell me they take an interest in occult sciences?' He slipped in.

'Tut! Tut! … . Occult Sciences, those are big words! The methods of these ladies are not exactly scientific! You occupy yourself in occultism, my dear sir?'

Lepicq was not there for a mild falsehood!

'It would be my keenest wish, dear lady! But … time. I am so rushed.'

'Of course! The hustle and bustle of Parisian life … .'

'However, because of my profession, I interest myself in physiognomy.'

He held forth on cranial bumps, conoidal or triangular faces, letting out several artless terms: amativity, affectionivity, acquisivity … .

'Dare I ask you to examine my cranium?' The widow said.

Lepicq did so without batting an eyelid.

'On the median section of the cerebellum cover I note a marked protuberance. Sign of family affection. Your maternal instinct is highly developed.'

'Alas!' The widow spoke with an expression suddenly distressed. I would have given everything to have a child!

16

That was denied me. Consider, Mr. Lepicq, that there will not even have been a miscarriage in my life!'

She resumed in a quieter voice: 'And what more do you see?'

'A weak alimentive bump. You must eat very little.'

'Like a bird!' The twenty-one stone widow murmured.

'Pronounced habitativity. Indicates love of one's home.'

They heard a noise of wheels. Mrs. Angat parted the curtains. They saw the young Lecorbin ladies magnificent as Artaban the Parthian king in their gig, but who all the same had not yet found husbands, ugly ducklings that they were!

'I'm interested in astrology,' the widow replied. 'It's enthralling! Knowing what astral fluids govern us, the means of counterbalancing harmful influences, what are our chances of success, and the epochs ... . Look! Me for example. I make no mystery there, I'm sixty years old. I was born 14 December 1876. The 14 December is accepted in the third star group configuration of Sagittarius, under the governance of Saturn. Saturn is an evil planet. In astrology we call it the Great Misfortune. Saturn scythes babies down, makes women sterile (here, a fresh sigh). In the main these subjects are neurosthenic, sickly ... .'

Lepicq had been unable to hold back a surprised look. Six feet three inches ... sixty-five inches round the waist ... twenty-one stone ... .

'But wait!' she spoke. 'First of all, Sagittarius is not bad, as a constellation. Ah! Indeed, it isn't as good as Virgo, but it's a deal better than Pisces! It gives love of the sciences, consistency of thought, calm passions. And I haven't told you the important thing. Do you know who entered into House I in my sky of nativity on the 14 December? Jupiter my dear sir! Now, what is House I? It's the House of Life. And what is Jupiter? It's the most beneficial of planets, it's the "Great Fortune"!'

'Yes, yes!' the lawyer, who was having great difficulty in keeping a straight face spoke. 'Yes, yes! Obviously!'

'Thursday is my lucky day; my colour, blue; my stone, turquoise; my perfume, saffron.'

Blue … . That was why the Jupiter-like room was decorated in blue! Why the blue satin disc was stuck in the angle of the window. And that was what this unusual perfume … .

The widow spoke of her married life. It had been brief. Three years, at the end of which an embolism had snatched Ernst Angat from his wife's affection. This premature death had not surprised Mrs. Angat; she had expected it ever since the study of her husband's sky of nativity had informed her that Angat was born under the sign of the Lion, which governs the heart. Saturn was his star group master. Mars, master of the day, added his violence to the sombre influences of Saturn, and Venus at right angles with Mercury in House VI (the House of Health) did not settle things.

Lepicq brought the conversation back to the ladies.

'My God,' said the widow, 'to be frank, these women amuse me! Each one has her way of discovering the unknown. Amandine Maisondieu the lines of the hand, Clemence Maisondieu dreams, Fernande Vasseur numbers, the butcher's wife Frelasset cards and coffee grounds.'

'Zélie Beluge?'

'She has a brain of a starling! She believes in all sorts of ridiculous formulae! In her head it's like in her shop window – a hotchpotch! But one forgives her everything; she's delightful!'

Lepicq uttered a word which enchanted the widow: 'All in all, these ladies dabble with the Sphinx!'

'To be fair,' concluded Mrs. Angat, 'I must point out a curious coincidence. Amandine Maisondieu had predicted to me the sudden death of my husband, following a study that she had made on the lines of his hand. At the base of the median, on the crest of Saturn, poor Angat carried a double cross. According to Amandine, this sign is not forgiving. I suppose she landed on it only by chance … .'

* * *

Swallowing his absinthe that evening, Lepicq asked himself if green, astrologically speaking, was lucky or unlucky for him. After dinner, he took a walk for his digestion, which unsurprisingly led him to the Patte-d'Oie-du-Petit-Roi.

Reine Coulemelle was removing her dress in front of a mirror. Lepicq saw her in a petticoat. She lived in a corner house overlooking the intersection of rue des Étourneaux and rue du Pot-de-Grés. Opposite her window rose a high wall. Not suspecting that anyone was able to observe her from the Patte-d'Oie, she was quietly attending to her toilet. She put on a different dress, a hat and prepared to go out.

Lepicq was tempted to wait and follow her but decided against it and resumed his walk. He went slowly up the slope and reached the plateau.

The air seemed to him trembling with radiations which, some falling vertically, others obliquely, all converged towards him. What a tangle of influences, what a jumble of mysterious powers!

The lawyer reflected on the effects of the planets combined perhaps with those of the stars, the clusters of the Milky Way, and those of the millions of spiral nebulae, islands of the Universe gyrating in infinity like Bengal fires, for the satisfaction of a pyrotechnologist who was not concerned with the expense!

He went back down the slope and crossed by the Patte-d'Oie again. In front of her wardrobe Reine Coulemelle took off her dress and hat.

'She's back in "her place." Her trip hasn't been long'

He returned to the hotel and went into his room just in time to pick up the end of a coded conversation between Médéric Plainchant and Zélie Beluge.

107, the woman from the *Wish to Please* telegraphed.

50 responded the man from the *Good Swordsman*.

The following day at the widow's home Lepicq was making the acquaintance of Fernande Vasseur, as expected. Shortly afterwards a woman with a threatening bosom, cheeks the colour of beefsteak, and who smelled of blood and suet arrived. She was Angèle Frelasset the butcher's wife.

'I'll start making tea?' Noémi asked.

'A moment, my girl,' the widow spoke. 'I only half expect the Maisondieus, but we will certainly have Zélie Beluge.'

'Good!' The servant agreed. 'I'm going to wait a little.'

She had scarcely said that when two timid knocks were struck on the front door.

'That's our Zélie!'

Under white hair a face as pink as a small apple, delicately bloomed like an August peach. Impulsive, merry, the behaviour of this sexagenarian, her gestures, her voice reminded one of a young girl. A hairstyle with a head-band emphasised this impression. And her eyes – a candid blue….

She began her childishness on the doorstep! They saw her bend down to slide the point of a hatpin into a gap in the floorboards and produce a pinch of dust which she gathered up and then threw at the wainscot, saying '*Ada*!'

She had seen a spider. This was not a good omen. But the word '*Ada*' has the power to chase off the bad spell!

Beluge had recipes of this calibre for all of life's situations! She said '*Esoenareth*!' to heal burns. '*Strugole Decutinem*' repeated three times warded off toothache. '*Valeam Albunazar*' was a sovereign remedy against colic.

'You don't know the news?'

'Yes!' The widow answered. 'We know!'

'Ah!'

Zélie Beluge's eyelids fluttered vigorously in front of her porcelain eyes.

'Ah well, yes!' The widow spoke again. 'Andréa Gauric has lost her case against Gratoulet!'

'I knew very well that you didn't know! It's not a question of Andréa! The Plantin woman ... .'

'Mary, from rue du Havre?'

'No! Irma, from rue du Plateau ... . The wife of the borough surveyor ... . Ah well, that's it!'

The women were seized with a sudden excitement.

'No? Say again?' ... . 'Ah, my word!' And ... . 'That went off well?'

'I'm sure that it's a young man!' Angèle Frelasset threw out. 'The coffee grounds assured me!'

'Absolutely not! It's a chit of a girl!'

'Good Lord!' The widow was in raptures. 'I must draw up the horoscope of this little angel! I, who have just got started building Mr. Lepicq's sky of nativity! There's a lot on my plate!'

She clapped her hands.

'Noémi, I think the Maisondieus will not be coming. You can make tea.'

'Tea is ready!' Noémi replied. She was not very taken with the Maisondieus and had not judged it useful to wait for them anymore.

Lepicq was standing close to the window. He saw a bent old man, whom he had not yet had occasion to notice, passing on the Square.

'Who's that old figure?'

The widow's face was scornful. The features of the other women, including Zélie Beluge, were expressing the same severity. Surprised, Lepicq repeated his question.

'Who's that?'

'No-one!' The widow answered curtly. 'It's Mr. Jaufre.'

At that point three peremptory knocks were struck.

With a wry look Noémi went to see. They heard the noise of walking sticks in the hall. The sitting room door opened.

21

'My God!' Lepicq thought with a start. 'Who are these birds of ill omen?'

These 'birds' were the two Maisondieu sisters.

CHAPTER 4

THE 800 FRANCS OF MR. JAUFRE

'Who have these ladies had the misfortune to lose?' The lawyer discreetly asked Mrs. Angat, indicating the Maisondieus in full mourning.

'Their mother and their father, taken away within three weeks of each other.'

'That's awful!'

Lepicq transferred his gaze with less hostility onto the two sisters. He tried to rekindle feelings of compassion in himself – in vain! It was not possible! They were too sinister! Incapable they said, of other attitudes, of expressions other than those which indicated grief. These long moustached old daughters, stiff, pinched, inspired him near to horror. It was a little as though the temperature of the room had abruptly dropped several degrees. The Maisondieus literally radiated chilliness.

Moreover, in their manner Lepicq **found** he didn't know what, strangeness, affectation, a disturbing absence of normality! … .

'These two bereavements, they happened recently ?' He asked further.

'It will be exactly twenty-four years in November that the mother and father Maisondieu died!' Mrs. Angat whispered, with a silent smile,

Lepicq was startled. Twenty-four years! It explained his impression, this ostentatious side, spectacular, aggressive, that he had sensed in their manner of wearing grief. Twenty-four years since they had taken to black, and had not given it up! Twenty-four years of dressing themselves only in sombre materials, of letting these haughty crepe veils flutter! Twenty-four years of parading this desolate look, of abstaining from any smiles, to make the rounds only as living images of Suffering, and taking on these postures of cemetery marble! They had settled with dignity into the funereal … .

Twenty-four years! … . That makes how many days? How many hours?

'It's sadism!'

The two sisters looked very alike. However, this likeness was more or less striking depending on the time of day.

The elder, Amandine, awoke each dawn with a tired face, crumpled and puffed up, but as the day wore on the pockets filled up, the wrinkles filled in and the creases faded; the look became less gloomy, came alive and ended up with a hard gleam. With Clémence the opposite happened. She awoke fresh, but each minute which passed violated this freshness, withered her, each hour her colour faded more. The afternoon hollowed her cheeks, twilight made her eyelids purple, enlarging a ring around her eyes which gradually died away. So that by evening Clémence was the true picture of Amandine on waking, and in the evening, Amandine the exact image of Clémence on waking! So that it was towards the middle of the day that they both had the same look, one starting to become weary while the other beginning not to be; they met up in a kind of middle state. It was realising this that the idea came to one that there must be one second, around midday, one tiny fraction of time when the two sisters resembled each other absolutely!

Amandine was born on the third of October under the sign of Libra, Saturn being the master of this decan. She was almost seventy years of age. Clémence had come into the world two years later, almost to the day, the fifth of October, and so was under the same sign and in the same decan as her sister.

24

Skinny, stooped, greyish skins, thin lips, sharp chins, rigid morals, suspicious, experts in hypocrisy, flaunting noble airs in public but, when alone, sifting through observations full of sourness, revelling in the most mean-minded quarrels, they were two perfect Saturnians!

'In my shop,' Fernande Vasseur was saying to Lepicq, 'I have a ladder with four steps. If I don't go up it fifty times in the day, I don't go up it once! Two hundred steps a day! Taking only three hundred days in the year, that makes six thousand steps! At twenty-five centimetres to the step, that gives fifteen hundred metres. Five times the height of the Eiffel Tower!'

On the Square, Mr. Jauffre dragged himself along at a snail's pace.

He was hardly prepossessing! Mr. Jauffre was a short old figure with weak features and trembling cheeks. His flesh seemed to have the consistency of jelly. One was tempted to say of him what one said of Camembert – that he was fully ripe! The head, completely bald, and which one imagined soft like the face, extended a huge forehead out of proportion. Small, black and very lively, his eyes revealed at certain times an anxiety going as far as to impress on his face an abject look.

'What does he live on?'

'Begging,' Frelasset spoke with disdain. 'He lives at other people's expense. The worst of leeches!'

'It's not begging that one must speak of!' Amandine threw out with hatred. 'It's swindling!' Lepicq wanted details.

'Well,' the widow spoke – with less spitefulness since Jupiter confers on its subjects indulgence and generosity – 'ah well, as you will see, he's going to pocket *our* money!'

Bit by bit the lawyer learned the whole story.

Jauffre had had in his time an interesting job in Registration at Havre. But he had to leave this post before having the right even to a part pension.

'Why was that?'

'Ah, that's it! … '.

They sniggered in an underhand manner.

They did not utter words of forced resignation, or about embezzlement, but Lepicq read their lips.

'He dipped into the till? He shut his eyes to fraudulent acts, in return for a good back-hander?'

Vague gestures, hesitant looks … . They could say nothing too definite. In any case they did not care to say precisely.

After that Jauffre had lived here and there on God knows what! Then, old age coming on, he had returned to install himself in Criquebec, the village of his birth.

It was then that he had demonstrated the extent of his shrewdness. Jauffre owned two houses in Criquebec. One of them, a blackish dump whose roof was held on by a miracle, happened to be on the Square. This was where he lived. The other, huge, with outbuildings and garden, rose above the plateau. Jauffre had managed to persuade the mayor, that arrogant Lecorbin, that it would be easy – and how complimentary for Criquebec! – to convert these buildings into a Retirement Home for the aged poor. He offered to donate the building to the town.

When one says 'donate', it's a question of what you mean! Jaufre *donated* the entire and permanent ownership of his house against a life annuity of eight hundred francs per month which would be paid to him up until his death. Lecorbin had accepted! He had forced the hand of the municipal councillors – of whom six were his creatures. Lecorbin was an ambitious man! Politics turned his head; he had his eye on nothing less than the Palais-Bourbon! For that, first becoming councillor general … . In this way his ridiculous projects were explained – the central boundary marker on the Square, which served only as a seat for the mute Barnaby to sit on! Near the church this Pump that no-one used, they had quite enough wells in Criquebec! A laughable Tourist Office, they were still waiting for the first tourist brought to this Office!

The project of the Retirement Home had always seemed to Lecorbin to serve his plans and the business had been completed. A ruinous affair … . First of all, the repairs which had cost an arm and a leg (weren't the architect and the building contractor serious political operators? So …). Then fitting out – furniture, beds, sheets, a refectory with all it needed, tables, chairs and so on …. the whole lot at exorbitant rates! Added to that the loss of earnings that the town was subjected to because this house no longer brought in taxes! Fourthly, the wages of Amédée Brot, warden of the Retirement Home who, by way of occupation, had only to twiddle his thumbs, because for the ten years that this demented bargain had been made, and in the six years since the hospice was set up, not one old man, not one old woman in Criquebec had agreed to cross the threshold, preferring their independence in the way that they understood! And is being in need a reason for renouncing one's dignity? So there was a nursing home that had served no purpose! And for ten years Jauffre regularly went every month to the taxman Gratoulet's till to get his eight hundred francs! Nine thousand six hundred francs per year! The Retirement Home had already cost Criquebec eighty thousand francs! And this wasn't the end of it!

Because – letting himself die, him? Not so stupid! With his appearance of geriatric ruin, his expression which said 'one foot in the grave, and the other close behind' – Jauffre kept going, taking good care of himself!

* * *

The Éphémérides of Raphaël in hand, the widow Angat had studied her Sky of Nativity, its dominant planet and the various positions of its luminaries in the zodiacal Houses, the whole lot in great detail. The result was not exactly cheerful! A triple signing of Saturn, Mars and Mercury in twelve-sided aspect, with lunar sub-signing; that signified unusual predispositions to perversity. Moreover Jupiter, as the particularly well-established major planet in the House of Health, guaranteed to this cunning Jauffre a scandalous longevity!

The only consolation for the people of Criquebec was that Lecorbin, in spite of his boundary marker, his pump, his Tourist Office and his rest home, was still not councillor general!

Noémi had served tea and cakes. The widow had filled the cups. Zélie Beluge was eating a macaroon, sucking a mousseline biscuit, gnawing a petit-beurre, with the greediness of a small girl.

'God! How unwell I feel,' Clémence Maisondieu moaned from time to time. And she took from her bag, which smelled horribly of medication, a box of pills of which she swallowed two or three or granules, or a flask of smelling salts. This old girl was a walking pharmacy!

'Pay no attention to it!' The widow whispered in Lepicq's ear. 'It's always the same refrain! She sees germs everywhere, she maintains that they are seeking to poison her; she's always at the point of death! But above all it's her imagination that's sick!'

'Tell me, my good Angat,' Clemence spoke at this moment. 'The last time we went to Yvetot you recall … .'

'Seeing that I'm telling you again that it was yellow!' Amandine cut in.

Both of them had a masculine voice. They nervously tapped the heads of their black-tasselled canes with bony fingers.

Clémence ignored the interruption.

'… You remember the colour of this cat that the auctioneer chased from the saleroom? Amandine maintains that it was yellow. Me, I see a black one, speckled with white.'

'I would see grey rather,' the widow said. 'But what is the interest?'

'I dreamed of a yellow cat, last night. It scratched me. Usually, this dream foretells a serious illness. Of course, if Yvetot's cat was yellow, that would explain my dream.'

'Ah well, perhaps it was greyish yellow after all!' The widow conceded. 'Yes, that must be it.'

'You're saying that to set my mind at rest!'

'If in doubt,' concluded Zélie, 'I would burn a handful of nettles this evening, Clémence, if I were you! That chases away the bad dream.'

Amandine Maisondieu was watching Prosper Lepicq's hands with a rather greedy look. Each time the lawyer raised his cup or put a cake in his mouth, she tried to see his palm.

These hands … . His hands in the hollows of which were written the man's character, his qualities and defects, even vices, his past, his future … .

'You have a very interesting hand, Mr. Lepicq. Passionate and intellectual!'

The only response from the lawyer was a smile.

For want of something better, Amandine began to study the fingers. 'Long and spatulate,' she said to herself, 'aesthetic tendencies. Slanting towards the index finger – reasoned ambition, directed. But the length of the first joint betrays an excessive tendency to fantasy, and the gap at the base of the fingers indicates prodigality, scorn of money. The opening at the thumb declares a disdain of conventions.'

Lepicq was dying for a smoke.

To his surprise he saw Clémence pull from her bag a cigarette case and matches. The eternally moribund liked tobacco! He slipped a hand into his pocket and pulled out a packet of Gauloise bleues.

But Clémence: 'Oh, sir … . Dare I pray you don't smoke? The fumes tear at my bronchial tubes!'

Flabbergasted, Lepicq made his Gauloises disappear.

'I could happily offer you mine,' said Clémence. 'Only ... .'

'Very gladly!' Lepicq burst out quickly putting out his hand. 'I don't know this brand. They are Polish? The cardboard tip'

'No, sir. Eucalyptus cigarettes.'

Lepicq withdrew his hand faster than he had put it out.

Amandine smiled. Thanks to the action, she had been able to see the upper part of the palm: Lepicq's heart line was broken, and branched: a flighty lad! Little constancy in his love affairs. But what a splendid head line he had!

The widow rose.

'Ladies ... . If you're quite happy, we are going through into the Uranus room.'

CHAPTER 5

THE INVISIBLE OLD LADIES

Each room in the widow Angat's house was placed under the invocation of a planet. The bedroom was dedicated to Venus, signifying beauty, softness, charm, gaiety and seduction. The dining room was under the sign of the Sun which is a very beneficial 'planet' astrologically speaking. The widow dealt with her business affairs only in the Mercury room, whose influence kindled her natural commercial acumen, a knowing sense of her interests which allowed Mrs. Angat to sniff out from a mile away the craftiness of her tenants.

Noémi slept in the Moon room; this suited her well, ancient lunatic that she was! Mars and Neptune were rooms for friends. The wicked Saturn had been downgraded into a glory hole where discarded objects were piled, unwanted trunks, broken furniture, old rags: all the rickety, all the moth-eaten, all the mildewed of a household that one keeps only because not throwing anything away is the first of the principles which makes for 'sound homes'. Finally, as to the planet Pluto, whose astrology has preoccupied her only recently, the widow had found it by chance a place in the kitchen, leaving her to use it more judiciously just in case one could be in a position of defining its influence on human destiny.

The house with ten rooms contained twelve windows, as though intentionally as many as there are constellations in the astrological firmament. Of course, each window had been dedicated to one constellation. The Pisces window, malign constellation, was a skylight feebly illuminating the storeroom of Saturn the baleful.

The widow rarely went into this storeroom, and she avoided like the plague putting her nose to the skylight. Noémi on the other hand, passed hours in this beastly place, raking about, and fond of planting herself at the skylight which looked over the interior of the Gentils. It has to be said that Noémi was an out-and-out sceptic! She stuffed into the same compartment the Stars, Pins, Lines of the hand, coffee grounds, dreams, egg yokes, ink blots, and numbers! Not that she did not have deep down her belief like everyone! She had. 'Certainly there are things!' She said. She believed in Zélie's formulae − spider's web for cuts, *Strugole Decutinem* against raging toothache, *Valeam Albunazar* against colic. She also believed in the Cards. But in the good and honest cards of piquet − the 32; not in the 78 cards of Frelasset, where bizarre figures were painted − the Juggler, the Devil, the Pope, the Fool, the Coins, the Swords, the card cutting, the Rods ... . Rather too complicated, this clutter! Especially, she did not believe in the virtues of their manipulation by the butcher's wife. Frelasset was not skilful: each to his own.

At Havre, where she took herself three or four times a year to visit a parent, Noémi knew an officially recognised fortune teller, Mrs. Adolphe, an extraordinary blind clairvoyant. Mrs. Adolphe told you the future in everyday language. '1.2.3.4.5. What's this card?'

'The king of clubs,' Noémi replied. She had really to lend her eyes to the clairvoyant since the latter was blind!

'The king of clubs,' repeated Mrs. Adolphe. 'That's a dark man.' She started her matching up again. '1.2.3.4.5. What's this?'

'The queen of hearts,' Noémi replied.

'Ah ah!' Mrs. Adolphe answered. 'A blonde woman! 1.2.3.4.5. What are you seeing?'

'The eight of clubs.'

'Money for you,' Mrs. Adolphe assured her. 'It will come to you from a dark man linked to a blond woman, or I am much mistaken! Look into your relationships, you will certainly see that this is so!'

Noémi smiled. 'I believe that I see who it is!' In fact, she did not have to look far to find the dark man! It was that Gratoulet the lewd tax collector! The blonde woman, that was Mrs. Aimée Gentil, the pharmacist's wife. On occasions Gratoulet, passing Noémi's room, gave her a commission for Mrs. Aimée: 'Tomorrow, such and such a time, such and such a place!' Mr. Paul Gentil, the husband, had not twigged! What mischief was there?

In addition, Noémi knew a deaf-mute in Yvetot. He hung out near the poultry market. Noémi never missed going to see him on each of her trips. This deaf-mute would offer envelopes on which he had marked in wax crayon:

Gentlemen and Ladies,
I am a deaf-mute
This envelope contains a 'Good Luck Letter'
Price free, please

'Pick me a good one!' Noémi said. She tendered ten sous. The deaf-mute was happy. Noémi too, because almost everything that was said in the good luck letter was true.

Aside from that, Noémi was an accomplished sceptic. It is why she persisted in christening the dozen windows of her mistress's as names of the months rather than as the names of the constellations.

'Madam, this morning the kids smashed the tile at the bottom left of the June window!'

The widow had to give herself over to calculations! 'June. Sixth month. The sixth constellation is that of Virgo. The window of the Virgo is in the Venus room.' Mrs. Delphine Angat translated. 'They have broken a tile in my bedroom!'

The smoke of Clémence's eucalyptus cigarette had rendered the atmosphere of the Jupiter salon stifling.

Lepicq took himself towards the Uranus room with a satisfaction tinged with curiosity. To what strange goings-on did these women reckon to abandon themselves?

If the lawyer had been even slightly interested in understanding astrology, he would not have had to ask himself this question. Uranus governs magnetic fluidity. This planet arouses and fortifies the astrological vocation of mediums. Can you imagine a place more favourable for table-turning?

Long net curtains hung in front of the two windows of the Uranus room. 'The Libra window and the Gemini window,' the widow said. 'The July window and the March window,' Noémi corrected. At the centre of the room the Table. Flimsy, round and with unique feet; an excellent table for what the women wanted to do.

'A moment,' said Clémence Maisondieu. 'What's the time?'

'Ten past five.'

'God! I was forgetting my pills!'

She ran to the kitchen, asked Noémi for a little water and let fall into it five drops of a colourless liquid. It was a remedy for hypertension.

She returned to the Uranus room. The moment had come for the women to make themselves invisible.

This operation is achieved by several procedures. The best – used by all the women of the region that age and rheumatism nail into an armchair – consists in putting themselves open to view. They position themselves near a window and remain still. Little by little the phenomenon happens. It needs a lot of patience. Indispensable conditions are immobility and continuous silence. By dint of catching the retina at any time anyone looks towards them, these images of the old ladies end up by the retinas no longer showing them up. *Always is the same as never.* Forever seeing a face in the same spot amounts to ceasing to see it, losing even the ability of noticing its presence at that spot.

It's so true that human beings only maintain themselves in the visible state thanks to a triple stratagem: movement, noise and, from time to time, absence … .

However, in the Uranus room the women used a very expeditious procedure to make themselves invisible.

The widow began by closing the shutters. After that, behind the net curtains, she drew thick, chestnut double curtains and, behind the curtains even thicker drapes of black velvet.

From then on, whatever the strength of the sunlight on the Square, the room was plunged into a satisfactory obscurity. With a sureness of movements and gestures conferred on them from long practice, the ladies took their places in immutable order around the table. Hands flattened, little fingers searching, touching, knitting together, to establish fluid contact.

'Let's concentrate,' the twenty-one stone widow recommended in a muffled voice.

Lepicq found himself between Zélie Beluge and Amandine Maisondieu. His left little finger was touching the right little finger of Zélie. To think that it was because of this sexagenarian with the ways of a child that he found himself in this ridiculous situation! All this because he had promised himself to uncover the secret of the conversations through numbers that were exchanged between the podgy cutler of the *Good Swordsman* and the impulsive seller of jokes and tricks of *The Wish to Please!*

'Let us concentrate!' The widow repeated.

Zélie's little finger was deliciously warm. Lepicq felt it supple, restless with a gentle trembling, the very fluttering of life. Amandine's little finger, on the other hand, was icy, stiff and dead. One made out clearly the noise of breathing; that of Vasseur was wheezy, a remnant of bronchitis … .

'I suggest … ,' murmured Frelasset.

35

'Sh!' The widow cut in. 'Think of your departed ones.'
A long silence, a tense silence, criss-crossed with boosts from all these wills. And the elemental Forces continuing to act, for the table took off. It took off briskly, impetuously.

'It's going to be a good séance,' the widow reflected, delighted.

Regrettably, in this religious ambience, they noticed a chewing noise – Clémence Maisondieu was munching a sugar-coated laxative. But these profane crunchings did not compromise the spirit of the table. Swamped with occult electricity it turned smoothly round. It was magnificent!

Respectfully, the widow enquired:

'Spirit, do you want us to agree that you will answer by one knock for yes and two knocks for no?'

The spirit knocked once – agreeing. Whose was it? Everyone had called up their own.

'Is it you? Ernest? Is it you my poor Angat?' The widow demanded softly.

Two knocks.

It wasn't Ernest Angat.

'Is it you, father?' asked Clémence Maisondieu.

One knock.

It was the late Marcellin Maisondieu. The sisters let out a sigh of triumph. It was *their* departed one who had come! It was moreover good to see that Marcellin Maisondieu had not complied with the combined call of his daughters!

'Father, are you able to make known to us whether ....'

'Excuse me!' Amandine cut in curtly. 'Leave me to speak to him, can you?'

'But ... .'

'I'm the elder! You question him afterwards!'

She asked: 'Father, do you experience bliss in the other world?'

This was disconcerting. Marcellin's spirit replied first with one knock, that's yes. Then, before they were able to follow up the interrogation, it knocked again. Two knocks this time. That's no. What to conclude from this ambiguous response? The spirit knew bliss, yes or no? Perhaps he wanted to signify Yes and No. To remain evasive and reticent, good Norman that he had been?

'Are you enduring sorrows?'

'No!'

'It's my turn!' Clémence spoke.

'Let me at least … .'

'He was my father as well as yours! As long as we have him, I maintain … .' And without any pause: 'Father, do you regret your earthly life?'

'No!' The late Marcellin spoke clearly.

'Do you know the fate of our mother on the other side?'

'Yes.'

'And is she near you?'

'No.'

'Are you suffering from this separation?'

Two emphatic knocks: 'No!'

'Father, are you able to reveal to us whether Hell really exists?'

'Yes.'

'Do you want to tell us that Hell really exists?'

'Yes.'

'Where is it?' Zélie Beluge threw out naively. Then, appreciating that the late Maisondieu wasn't able to respond to a question put like that, she explained:

'Hell is down below?'

'No.'

'High up, then?'

'No.'

'On earth?' Prosper Lepicq asked in a cavernous voice which gave the women goose bumps.

'Yes,' declared the late Marcellin Maisondieu.

'Father,' Clémence resumed, 'tell us … .'

'You're taking advantage!' Amandine observed. 'Me now, if you'll allow!'

37

At every séance they argued, fought over their family ghosts, which they plagued and harrassed … .

'Are you able to reveal your future?'

'Yes'

'Do you wish to?'

'No.'

'I don't know why father,' Amandine spoke plaintively, 'but it seems to me that you're not …. .' (She dared not say: Not good-humoured …). She said, 'not happy?'

'No,' said Marcellin

'Aren't you thrilled to speak to your children?' Amandine replied sternly.

Marcellin Maisondieu hesitated. In the course of his earthly life his daughters had tyrannised him with a constancy which had made of his gentle nature a slave subjugated to all their wishes. And even now they refused to leave him at peace! Their anger seemed to frighten him! However, he found the courage to reply frankly, if weakly:

'No.'

The widow Angat interrupted. With her usual tact, she killed at source the domestic dispute:

'Perhaps,' she suggested, 'what they claim is true − that by summoning up the spirits we are holding them back, delaying their accession to a more perfect state?'

'Yes!' Marcellin replied with fury, given that it was permitted to judge the strength of his feelings from the vigour with which the blows were struck.

After that, the table fell back as though dead.

'Ah well, that went admirably!' The widow rejoiced, opening the curtains. 'It's by far our best séance!'

'Ye-es!' Amandine let out, giving the table a suspicious look. 'But have you noticed? The table was turning from left to right whereas, in principle, tables turn from right to left, like the stars, to obey the cosmic law … .'

'Bah!' Said Vasseur, 'exception proves the rule!'

Lepicq had put on his most ingenuous air but, deep

inside he said to himself:

'Go on! I blundered!'

For truth to tell the lawyer, assisted by his thumbs, the flat of his hands, his right knee and the toe of his left shoe, had imposed promptings on the light table which had been, for the late Maisondieu, an invaluable help!

The ladies chatted a little longer in the Jupiter room.

★ ★ ★

On the Square the young girls were now playing at ball against the wall. They were heard reciting: '*No moving. No laughing. One hand. The other. One foot. The other. In front. Behind. In front. Behind. In front behind. Behind in front. In front behind in front. Behind in front behind. Flyswat. Little roll. Big roll. And France!*'

Abruptly, more sounds! Lepicq, surprised, took himself to the window and with the tip of his index finger, separated the curtain a centimetre. He had already picked up the traditional gesture!

'Hullo!' He said. 'Mr Jaufre. He's coming back to Gratoulet's place with his eight hundred francs! "His" eight hundred francs ... That's to say "our" eight hundred francs!'

With this money, this lovely money that everyone had so much trouble getting hold of, Jaufre was going to live off the fat of the land for an entire month! He was going to pay for drinks for his friend the wicked mute Barnaby. He was going to buy calvados for Genêtou the mayor's secretary, and for Doré the senior clerk of Mr. Figuier the solicitor. Genêtou ... Doré ... . Two serious-minded family men but thirsty, boozers who let themselves be led by their mouth and who have been taken to the edge with a small glass! If they had had a scrap of self-esteem, would they have agreed to sit down in low dives, little used by the decorous of Criquebec, at Jaufre's table clinking glasses with this old bandit?

The former clerk of the Registration Department dragged himself along under the bright light. His yellow jacket gave him the look of a large cockchafer. He wore a Panama burned by the suns of ten summers. His trousers were so worn they no longer had a colour. His shoes had lost their heels years ago. A fine citizen!

It was the passing by of this villainous old man which had silenced the young girls. Because the children were raised with scorn and dislike of Jaufre, the exploiter of Criquebec. Jaufre who, each month, metaphorically speaking, introduced himself so to speak into your house, under your roof, slipping his hand into your pocket, withdrawing your purse and ironically taking from it a tidy forty sous coin. There were four hundred souls in Criquebec. At two francs a head that added up! And then he'd sneak away at a leisurely pace, with a nasty little grin which meant 'I'll be back in a month! Have no fear, I won't forget! And it will go on for a long time, a long time … . Oh! You haven't finished stumping up your two francs every thirty days! I have a hard life! Before they put me into the ground, there are a good many in Criquebec who will have been driven to the cemetery! It's all the same to me, The parents dead, the sons will pay! Let's hope I have my eight hundred francs!' Crook!

★ ★ ★

Amandine Maisondieu's glances often settled on Prosper Lepicq's hands. Unconsciously, the lawyer had closed his fingers, as though under a defiant reflex action. His grip clenched on the life line, the line of fortune, the liver line, the lust line, the girdle of Venus, and the great plain of the palm, and the mountains, and the triangles which signify ability, the round halos which suggest success, the forks, a good indicator if they are in the ascendant and, if the opposite, indices of setbacks, the crescents which betray

40

inconstancy. The gratings, synonymous with obstacles, the squares which reveal energy, the spots, lucky or unlucky according to their colour and position, the crosses which rarely indicate good, and the stars which denote inescapable fatalities ... . So what the old crow had wanted was to loosen his fists, to decipher there Destiny's hieroglyphics, the secrets of mind and heart ... . But Lepicq, fingers tightly clenched like a child playing with another at 'How many marbles in my hand,?' was seeming to say 'Work it out!'

More exaggerated politeness and the two funereal sisters took their leave and went off. In low voices they squabbled over domestic questions, tapping the dry ground roughly with the ends of their canes. Couril the dwarf made a detour so as not to find himself in their path. Strange silhouettes, tall, sombre, solemn, elegant like ... .

'Like cypresses!' Lepicq said to himself.

Even so, this thought did not give him an inclination to smile. He decided he'd had enough of this circle of loonies, of this atmosphere of farce! It was far too stupid! Even the mystery of the coded messages had ceased to preoccupy him. The devil take it! He was on holiday! The road was calling him, the road which stretched out lazily between the blessed plains and the woods which dozed in the heat!

'Setting out! ... '.

Just then, Angèle Frelasset was announcing word of a journey. In the morning she had consulted the needles. An oblique line cutting two undulating lines had put her on guard 'Abandon a dangerous trip.' She, who was reckoning to take herself to Havre in the course of the coming week... .

The Maisondieu sisters had disappeared. Amandine at the far end of the Square had shut herself into the big family residence of the Maisondieus of which as the elder she had possession.

Clémence, went up towards her house by the rue de l'Église, much smaller than that of her sister. This property had been given as dowry by Adrienne Maisondieu, née Séverin, at the time of her marriage with Marcellin Maisondieu.

'You could do a good thing, Angèle,' advised Zélie. 'Collect an oak leaf at full moon. Make yourself a little scapula, shut the leaf in it and carry it on your bosom, next to your skin. I do it myself. It's a marvellous protection!'

'I certainly will do it,' assured the butcher's wife kindly.

Inside, she was laughing at this recipe for mumbo-jumbo and thinking that when she was at home that evening playing patience with the Tarot cards, Chien de Pique, or Discovery, it would be the very devil if she did not get the facts for avoiding this trip. And, if the games of patience did not speak, she would consult the ink blots, the coffee grounds, the egg yolk. She would go as far as molten lead if it was necessary! She did not lack the means for information!

Fernande Vasseur was impatient to know what Christian name Irmam Plantin of the rue du Plateau was intending to give to her baby. As soon as she could know it she would calculate the personal Number of this little girl and, from the Table of numerical Conformity of the Hand of Fatima, she could come up with an idea of her chances of success in life.

The widow Angat was also reflecting on the newborn, for whom she was impatient to draw up her astrological horoscope; not to mention the compilation of the sky of nativity of Mr. Prosper Lepicq – a really charming and gallant man, and a noble soul, be it said in passing!

They parted.

★ ★ ★

Lepicq sat on the terrace of the Pibole house. Barnaby, astride the boundary marker, was grumbling. That mute had to be born under the zodiacal sign which produced orators! Happily Saturn, really inspired for once, had tied his tongue!

The dwarf was tirelessly kicking out his legs one in front of the other and fixed into his large stomach like two beetroots in a pumpkin.

'Tomorrow morning I'm off,' Lepicq told himself.

He dined with a good appetite, then took a post-prandial stroll during which he carefully avoided the Patte-d'Oie-du-Petit-Roi. He was not at all keen to know whether the dwarf, this evening as on other evenings, was on lookout under the window of Reine Coulemelle, nor whether the postmistress was making herself beautiful in view of a nocturnal jaunt.

He returned, undressed in double-quick time with three movements.

Zélie Beluge and Médéric Plainchant were free to telegraph each other numbers as much as they wished; that didn't worry him any more.

He threw himself on the bed.

Time to count a hundred. He was asleep!

★ ★ ★

He woke up sprightly, with pins and needles in his legs. What a fine walk he was going to take in the fresh morning!

'I'm going to rejoin the Seine, passing along the left bank, and I'm lunching at Quillebeuf. That must be nice, Quillebeuf, from the name alone I should get an idea … .'

He checked his luggage – handkerchiefs, boxer shorts, shirts, jumpers, socks, slippers, bathing trunks, pyjamas, Montaigne – perfect!

He went downstairs. Mrs. Pibole made a long face .

'You're leaving us already Mr. Lawyer?'

'Ah yes! I'm going to Havre. Serve up my breakfast, and let me have my bill.'

At that moment, Augustin Pibole came in almost running. He was excessively agitated.

'An unusual thing has happened!'

'What then?'

'Old Jaufre … .'

'Well?'

'He's dead!'

'At last! … '. Mrs. Pibole exclaimed. 'You're making a lot of noise for nothing Augustin!' She added, acidly, 'Jaufre will not be carried off sorely regretted!'

'Yes, but hang on! That's not the best bit! Do you know how he died?'

'Well speak up, instead of poking your tongue at us,' the wife was impatient.

'They've murdered him!'

Lepicq breathed a long sigh, looked into space for some seconds, then gave Mrs. Pibole the case containing his luggage.

'Be kind enough to take that back up into my room. I'm no longer leaving.'

CHAPTER 6

THE FAMILY CIRCLE

Curled up on a bedside rug … .

It was in this position that Barnaby, this morning as each morning towards seven o'clock, come to see whether the old figure had entrusted to him a few trivial jobs, had found the body. Terrified, he had rushed on to the Square, knocking at doors, alerting everyone, attempting to make himself understood with a gesture, since it was impossible by word. He hit his neck, moaning 'Offe … Ou ou-o! Offe … Ou ou-o!' Someone smarter than the others had finished by understanding.

Jauffre had received a knife thrust in the neck.

He was lying on his left thigh, nose in waistcoat, fingers clenched on stomach. The jacket collar was soaked in blood. There was a large sticky brown stain on the rug.

In the summer everyone rose early in Criquebec. Already every one of the old ladies was at her post behind her window. The widow Angat, that heifer Amandine Maisondieu, that crow … . At the *Good Swordsman*, Plainchant was passing his nail over his knives. At the *Wish to Please*, Zélie Beluge was dusting the fancy goods and the trifles. The dwarf Couril was pacing the Square. The whole population was in good order … . Thereupon, like a bomb, this news which set off an excitement and changing the town into a mad anthill!

'The blade passed a few millimeters from the spinal column,' Dr. Pouacre declared.

'Death instantaneous?' The mayor enquired.

'Not necessarily. Death pangs may have needed five to ten minutes.'

To judge from the rigor mortis the crime went back some dozen hours. That's to say between six and eight o'clock the previous evening. The diagnosis was in line with what they knew of the habits of the dead man. Jaufre never went to bed much later than eight o'clock. On the other hand, a glance at the kitchen revealed that the old figure had still not eaten – a scrap of boiled meat on a plate, horseradish and an uncut round loaf on the oilcloth. Finally, this morning Barnaby had found the front door closed only on the latch.

'This business must have been done shortly after he'd returned from Gratoulet's place.'

The crime was simple to reconstruct.

The murderer let himself into Jaufre's house, doubtless through the back of the building. There was a courtyard giving on to the rue Marché-Couvert. The murderer goes up to the first floor, passes into the bedroom, hides himself between the wall and the bed behind the corded curtains which fall as a canopy to the ground. Jaufre in turn goes into this room. He wants to change his straw hat for a skullcap, his overcoat for a jacket and his boots for slippers.

He sits himself on the bed, a depression indicated this. He bends over to unlace his shoe. He presents his soft, fat, white neck. The murderer opens the curtains, stretches his arm. He can aim at leisure, striking a confident blow.

The weapon, a long kitchen knife, was lodged in the wound. On the base of the blade it was possible to see the maker's inscription: 'Mr. Plainchant'.

Jaufre's being dead, and quite dead, the doctor judged it pointless to transfer the body. Leaving things alone … . Lecorbin had called Yvetot by phone. The public prosecutor would be there before lunchtime.

'Touch nothing, if you please, gentlemen! One does not wish that. One can so soon wipe out a print, destroying evidence without suspecting it!'

They had respect for the gap in a particular door that they had found half open, the position of a particular chair standing askew; everything can have its importance. They moved around as though among eggs. On the other hand, it was so dirty, so revolting in Jaufre's house! It was not encouraging!

The house consisted of four main rooms. On the ground floor a dining room and an office, if one dared give this name to a room furnished with a chair and a rickety table, a piece of junkroom furniture gnawed by creepy crawlies and swollen with damp. The chair, table, the furniture were overloaded with grimy books and dog-eared papers. On the first floor the bedroom and 'library'. 'Library' was one way of expressing it! Shelving made by Barnaby out of old boxes. Books on geography, history and science, some more battered than others.

A narrow loft. The kitchen communicated with the cellar by a trapdoor from which a ladder emerged. In the yard a hut, acting as a woodshed.

As well as the mayor and the doctor, five people were present in the house: Mr. Figuier the solicitor, Doré his senior clerk, Genêtou the mayor's secretary, Aubin the village constable and Prosper Lepicq, whose card had served as introduction to the mayor. With the exception of the solicitor, everyone had a pitying look, but it was put on, it felt false. They were playing out a farce.

On the threshold a swelling crowd was crushed. All the inhabitants of Criquebec were mustered on the Square, like blood surging towards the heart at moments of strong emotion. The dominant feeling was astonishment. That the little town has been able to be the stage for a murder, it was not so much that! But that the victim was old Jaufre! The murderer had to be a first rate freak! And yet, it was not the absurd aspect of this crime that was scaring people. It was that Jaufre was dead. Was this credible? So he no longer existed! It was all over! They would not see him any more, every thirty days, slipping out of his dark house like a janitor, and creeping towards the tax office? The tale of the eight hundred francs per month, of the forty sous per head of population, was it in the past? ... . They had trouble believing that! A little as though by dint of hoping for the death of this old man who was scoffing at the tomb, they had come to regard him as immortal!

Another sentiment mingled with the amazement. Shame ... . The word is perhaps extravagant? An embarrassment, a discomfort of which they were aware only vaguely. Had Jaufre died in his bed of illness, or by accident on the Square, they would have found that fine, they would have said 'Ouf! Good riddance!' But like this! ... .Murdered! And what a villainous crime! A knife blade driven into his fat neck! He had bled just like a pig. All the people who over the years had wished, persistently, assiduously, the death of the exploitive Jaufre were feeling a grudge against the murderer, because of this manner that he had adopted of himself acting as the avenger for Criquebec, the servant of a population's hatred, the executor, the dispenser of justice! No-one had been charged with settling his account with Jaufre. However, they felt themselves vaguely backing the deed.

★ ★ ★

Genêtou and Doré each carried a leather briefcase. Doré's was black, Genêtou's fawn. The two men were around forty, with a similar physique, good bearing, the beginnings of a paunch, a ruddy face, bright eyed, strong breath (they had a liking for coffee with calvados and bottled cider!). Genêtou cultivated a bushy black moustache. They had a rather foolish air in this scene of blood. They followed their masters. Dr. Pouacre, not an ounce of pomposity, a man too pale with sluggish blood and relaxed. He had hurriedly slipped on his town trousers and a comfortable house jacket;

the first two buttons of his nightshirt were undone, showing three pathetic blond hairs in competition on his chest. By contrast, Mr Figuier was truly hirsute! His hair burst everywhere, it flowed in a cataract over the neck, gushed amazingly from the ears; the beard was eating up his eyes; the eyebrows, joined in a single ridge consumed his forehead, falling back down like a rake over his eyelids, long twisted hairs on wrists and fingers. This man of the law, the first shock abated, had adopted the manner appropriate to his calling; reserved, attentive, the brief word, the incisive glance, the impassive expression. Lecorbin was more encompassing! In his position as mayor, he represented not only the Law, Authority, Order, but also Justice — until the more qualified came to discharge this last concern. All arms and legs, this strapping fellow was already striving to construct hypotheses, build theories, fabricating only to himself the questions and answers, firing off every two minutes in his brassy voice: 'According to me … In my opinion … Me. I … Methinks … .' Great pity that his fellow citizens had not agreed to direct this living trumpet to Parliament! Those gentlemen of the National Assembly would have appreciated ferocity!

Lepicq experienced a curious feeling. A suspicion — nothing rational anyway. A purely instinctive state of alert. The more subtle side of his watchful nature warned: Attention! Eyes open! Something's going to happen … . But what? Upon whom in particular is it it advisable to keep an eye? The bawling mayor, the lethargic doctor, the cold solicitor, or the secretary and senior clerk because of their more than usually simple air — or finally, the village policeman Aubin planted on the doorstep facing the people of Criquebec?

Lepicq understood only later when there was no one left in the house of death.

These gentlemen had split up. Genêtou and Doré together went back up the rue de l'Église. In front of Jaufre's door, the village policeman on guard … . In small groups people debated. The dwarf Couril, solitary and silent as usual, wandered among the groups. At Pibole's, Barnaby, seated at a table in front of a bowlful of cider, was very popular and repeated endlessly his comical expressions: 'Offe … Ou Ou-o … .'

Lepicq dashed into the rue de l'Église. He walked very quickly. Past the first bend he saw again the senior clerk and the secretary. He drew closer. The two men were in discussion, like everyone else, but discreetly. Lepicq finally caught up with them. At that moment, Genêtou turned. No question of keeping a close watch! Lepicq offered a drink in a bar in Central Criquebec. Before they had ordered, the patron placed three small cups of coffee and a half-bottle of calvados on the table.

Genêtou and Doré had lost that inane air which had struck Lepicq so strongly. They were rather perky. A little too chirpy perhaps. 'Relieved … . Liberated … .' the lawyer told himself. His suspicions affirmed themselves. Something, God knows what, had happened in Jaufre's shanty … .

The briefcases of course! The black and the fawn briefcases! Classic trick: one puts the briefcase on the coveted item, and … hey presto! Doré and Genêtou had spirited something away from the old man's house. Moreover, the simple fact of having left their homes at seven o'clock in the morning, with their briefcases, was enough to prove … .

'Funny business!' Genêtou said.

They knew the lawyer's profession, but his name told them nothing. Lepicq presented himself with clarity, cited certain outstanding criminal cases in which he had revealed the solution before the police. The abduction of the priest Bertrant. The visions of Miss Dorothée F. Bridge. And the affair of the Phantom Speaker, which had set the whole of France laughing.

'Hang on then!' Doré exclaimed. 'It isn't you who untangled the crime of the Jardin des Plantes?'

'That's me.'

'Also, I was saying … You remember, Genêtou? The strangler! The Monster!'

'I'll say! Do I recall! Like that sir, that could be you, the celebrated … .'

'Well, yes! That's me, the celebrated … as you say!'

They had assumed their inane air again. They savoured their calvados slowly, nodding heads, feigning wonderment. But Lepicq diagnosed nervousness, discomfort. The briefcases were set down on his left on a free table. The bar was dark. For the time being no other customers but the three men.

'You are reckoning to involve yourself in this business, Mr. Lepicq?'

'Absolutely not! I'm on holiday.'

But the tone of voice signified 'Absolutely yes! What do you think I'm doing at this moment ?'

'You knew Jaufre well?' He asked.

'So-so … .'

(Naturally! They were in Normandy. To extract a clear yes or no, it needed the cross and the flag!)

Lepicq was recalling phrases heard the previous evening in the widow Angat's salon. 'Doré, Genêtou, serious-minded family men in work. But thirsty. Boozers who let themselves be led by their mouths … .'

They clinked glasses. Basically Jaufre was not so wicked as they made out.

'How did he occupy himself?'

'With nothing! He lived for the day.'

'You can't imagine for what reason … .'

'Someone killed him? Well, no! I don't know of his enemies.'

That was true. Jaufre was the object of four hundred deep-seated hatreds; general loathing weaved around him for ten years; a malign spider's web. But he hadn't what one calls an enemy.

51

'Not a farthing of savings … .'

'Wait a minute!' Genêtou retorted. 'He left Gratoulet's place with eight hundred francs. There are some for whom eight hundred francs is quite a sum!'

The briefcases … . Those two bursting briefcases … . All the same Lepicq was not able to order bluntly 'Open that for me! Show me what's inside!' He took a light-hearted tone. 'You start work early!'

'Pooh!' Doré spoke. 'Filing … .' He fiddled with the leather which squeaked. 'While it's on my mind, I must check whether I haven't forgotten … . Will you excuse me?'

And he opened it, the briefcase! He pulled out a pile of documents belonging to the project of Mr. Figuier. They were various deeds of very old apartments. All that, executed, ratified, settled, null and void, buried … . Archives.

And then in turn Genêtou opened his briefcase, letting roll out the bumf which he leafed through, grumbling about Lecorbin who felt from time to time the need to make him carry out searches on the hotchpotch of birth, marriage or death certificates, of land taxes, of statements, on arrests or of regulations fallen into disuse. All in the cause of his electoral ambitions! Lecorbin cared about giving himself the appearance of a busy mayor!

The mischief stuck out a mile! They had sensed Lepicq's suspicions and his curiosity concerning the briefcases. 'OK!' the wily birds had said to themselves! 'We're going to put the briefcases on show since they contain nothing of interest!' They had carried out this operation with an eagerness which betrayed them. Lepicq was certain at present that they had made something disappear from Jaufre's place. It was in their pockets that he would have to look.

He did not insist. Moreover, he had not wasted time. He had introduced himself into what he called 'the family circle.'

The objective that he aimed at in getting involved in

criminal activities he had himself defined many a time as:

'I look to discover the murderers so as to … offer them my services as a lawyer! My method? Very simple! Suppose that I have reason to think that the murderer is a part of the 'family circle' – in other words, that he is one of the associates of the locality where the crime was committed. I'm indifferent to who he is, but it is vital that he knows of my existence. He sees me at work. We have occasion to exchange remarks on the rain and the fine weather; he offers me a cigarette, I give him a light. It could happen that we meet up at the same table; that creates a cosy situation! When my investigations have shown me the guilt of my man, what more natural than saying to him, more or less: 'My good friend, I know everything! Oh, I have no intention of handing you over! I don't do that line, I'm a lawyer. But you have to foresee the worst. The police are perfectly capable of nicking you. In that case, don't you agree with me in admitting that I am the best suited man in France to defend you in front of a jury? I knew how to expose you; it's a guarantee that I will know how to save you! … . In general,' Lepicq concluded pleasantly, 'I'm a door-to-door salesman in crimes.'

Ah well, in Criquebec, the 'family circle' was beginning to define itself. And Lepicq was in there. With Doré and Genêtou the business was properly under way. He was sitting at the same table, they had clinked their glasses. Since they had a weakness for coffee and calvados the lawyer had promised himself to offer them as much as would be necessary!

Abruptly, a suspicion came to him: what if he had fooled himself? What if Doré and Genêtou, rather than seizing an object or a compromising document at Jaufre's place had, on the contrary, brought an item, a document designed to direct the enquiry along a false trail?

CHAPTER 7

THE POSTCARD

The gentlemen from the Public Prosecutor's Office made two discoveries straight away. No money in Jaufre's wallet. Nor in the wardrobe in the room, nor wherever it was, where the putting away of money was possible. They found no trace of the eight one hundred franc notes handed over to the old figure by the tax man.

So, strong presumptions then that theft had been the motive. Just as he had said to Genêtou 'There are some for whom it is a tidy sum, eight hundred francs!'

Second discovery: when the forensic doctor turned over the body he found a pencil on the carpet, and a postcard of Criquebec Square showing the boundary marker. On the section reserved for messages, numerals were lined up which, it seemed, were additions which had not been finished:

$$13 \quad 17 \quad 12$$
$$11 \quad 17 \quad 13$$

The judge reckoned that he did have good grounds for dwelling on this discovery – the old man had just received the money, he was preoccupied in some sort of matching up when the murderer had struck him.

Contrary to all hopes the initial investigations of the inspector, called Farjoux, and seconded from Rouen for the case, did not lead to the discovery of any sign, of any print. The murderer was a careful man. He had handled the knife with gloves or had wrapped his fingers in cloths.

The doctor, judge and clerk of court went up to refresh themselves at Lecorbin's place while the police officer was investigating. The latter was surprisingly agitated, as though on hot coals. His first concern was to run to the Pibole café and ask for a telephone link with Rouen. He let fly in a trembling voice: 'So? Anything new?'

He hung up with a relieved expression and explained to Pibole: 'I have my wife who's expecting a baby! You work out whether I'm amusing myself here!'

Interrogation of the mute was difficult. He understood the questions well enough, but it was impossible to catch the meaning of the squawking that came out of his throat! If only he had understood writing! … . Aubin, who had patience, took on the role of interpreter and they knew from this that the knife had never belonged to the victim. It had therefore been carried by the murderer. Unfortunately, knives of this model, were very common, Médéric Plainchant admitted to having sold a number of them. Moreover, the mute reckoned that he left Jaufre at around six o'clock the previous evening after work and had not seen him again that evening.

* * *

'13 + 17 + 12 = 42. 11 + 17 + 13 = 41. 42 multiplied by 41 gives 1722. I'm jumping 1000. See, 722 … .'

In the Jupiter room of the widow Angat, Vasseur combined the numerals listed on the postcard and referred to the numerical Table of Correspondence of the Hand of Fatima, to obtain their specific significance.

'700 means: Strength, vigour, health.'

'Mm! … . That hardly corresponds!'

22 was more interesting. Invention, prudence, mystery.

Vasseur resumed her calculations: '13 from 17 gives 4. 11 from 12 gives 1. 13 from 17 gives 4. 4 plus 4 equals 8, and 1: 9 means: Pains, sorrows, assassination attempt. I know very well that that proves nothing, but it's odd, don't you find?'

Indefatigable, she tried a new combination: 'There is twice 13. I admit that they cancel each other out. Twice 17. I'm also missing out. Remainder: 11 and 12. To the total: 23. 23, the numerical Table of Correspondences said: Calamity, Vengeance.'

'Ah well, but … '. Vasseur resumed. 'Perhaps they killed poor Jaufre through vengeance!'

Poor Jaufre … .

Already they were starting to speak of him with pity and sweetness. He wasn't worth a lot alive, but this horrible death! … .

Lepicq pretended to follow with interest the additions, subtractions, multiplications and divisions of Vasseur. He could have, and without doubt he ought to have run through the town as the inspector was doing, questioning, trying hard to untie tongues. He preferred to be here, with these mad old bats! He felt that, doing this, he was more in his line, pursuing more closely his technique. The Family Circle… . He reflected on the coded messages which were aimed, very early in the morning, very late in the evening , at Zélie Beluge and Médéric Plainchant.

'That night,' Clémence Maisondieu related, 'I saw myself in the middle of a rocky plain. The weather was stormy, I didn't have my umbrella, I said to myself "You are going to get drenched!" Just imagine that – I had to cross this large area by hopping!'

'It's extraordinary' the widow said, 'what the mind can invent when one is no longer there to keep it in hand!'

'Leaping by hopping was tiring me a lot. I made ten jumps, I changed feet, I made ten more jumps and I stopped. Well, my dear Angat, at each pause I saw a snake leave me from between my feet and fly away! According to the Egyptians Key of Gold, dreaming of snakes is a bad sign.'

She cast a glance at the miniature clock framed with a zodiacal circle: four o'clock. It was time for her pills. She brought out her flask and asked Noémi for a drop of water in a glass.

'Me,' said Zélie, 'I dreamed that my shoelace was untied, and then that I let an egg drop.'

'Broken egg,' Clémence explained. 'Misfortune. Shoelace which unties itself. Interesting information.'

'Good,' Zélie said. 'Jaufre's death! I've had the premonition of it! There my dream fades!'

On the matter of the crime, Angèle Frelasset had, in the morning, consulted the coffee grounds and the ink blots. The two were in agreement for indicating the murderer.

'Who is that?'

The butcher's wife hesitated to answer. Finally she said 'Couril.'

'Well,' the widow said, 'I could believe him wicked enough to give a nasty blow, but why would he have killed Jaufre? Not for 800 francs anyway!'

Couril had done well. He enjoyed at the very least 1500 francs of income per month. Without taking into account the taxes in kind which let him carry on his farming.

Zélie Beluge also had her method of divining. It was childish, like her recipes. It consisted in writing down on pieces of paper the names of people likely to be suspects and of throwing these papers into a container full of water, pronouncing a magic formula: *Aragoni Labilasse Eptalicon Parandamo Lamboured*. The first paper which floated was the correct one. This procedure had indicated Barnaby to her as the murderer.

'The mute could have let himself be tempted by 800 francs,' agreed Clémence.

Amandine Maisondieu remained silent. She had only

one method for predicting the future – palmistry.

'Ah,' Zélie said, 'if the police knew how to obtain *Quirium*! … .'

'Quirium? What's that.'

'An amazing stone. You lean it against someone's temple. Even if it goes against their interest, they are obliged to tell the truth!'

★ ★ ★

The heat was stifling. Everyone was shutting themselves away. Some were going as far as installing themselves in their cellar to taste the delights of a relative coolness. Farjoux was knocking on doors; he saw only half-dressed people. They invited him to come and sit down in front of iced cider in dining rooms with the shutters drawn. From the ceilings hung ribbons of sticky paper black with the bodies of flies. Farjoux was reflecting on his wife in Rouen, .. . He said to himself: 'Let's hope that they have really noted the telephone number of the café Pibole, so as to call me if something happens!'

He would have given much to find himself at his wife's bedside, instead of being here to hold an investigation on … . Good God on Jaufre, you know? This thought brought him back to the enquiry.

But the townsfolk knew nothing.

'No, we saw no-one speaking to old Jaufre yesterday evening. No, we saw no-one going into his place or coming out of it. Where were Mr. So-and-So and Mr. So-and-So, and Mrs. So-and-So? They hadn't noticed!'

Always this widespread tale of seeing nothing. They didn't present the thing in that light, they didn't use that word 'nothing'– but it came to the same thing.

'Mr So-and-So must have found himself on his doorstep … . Mrs. So-and-So must have found herself behind her window … .' They had to be. They always were! They were aware of it. They no longer paid attention.

'And Couril?'

'On the Square. He's always there as a rule.'

'What sort of character is he?'

People became reticent. They didn't like Couril. It was not unnoticed that at night he roamed about, with an air of watching … . He made stops here and there. In the vicinity of Patte-d'Oie-du-Petit-Roi for example he settled down! Which did not prevent his dashing off at speed when someone was approaching. Perhaps as well that he managed things … . Perhaps not … . In any case, he certainly had no connection with the crime. They said it for something to say.

'Of course! … . And Barnaby?'

'A miscreant.'

'Is that all?'

'A down-and-out, for whom one wishes kindness because he is disabled! He's not much liked though, that one!'

'He steals?'

'Possibly yes … . Possibly no … . Me, you see, I've never seen anything. I barricade my poultry in, I lock my wardrobe, I bolt my door. I sleep with my ears cocked!'

'Of course.'

'But there are those who complain of it … .'

'Of having been robbed?'

'Yes and no! That or something else.'

'In short – who complains!'

'Who?'

'Ah, certainly! … . There are those who complain all the time, you know how it is!'

Impossible to pin them down. Everywhere the same song: 'Saying that there are no apples, there are apples! But, to say that there are apples … .' All the more so since Farjoux was from the North. He didn't know how to take these Normans.

'And my wife, during this time …,' he said to himself.

59

'Heck! He had picked his moment well for murdering, that old fogey!'

He asked: 'Jaufre?' Smile. They hardly liked him either!

'Ah that! So they don't like anyone in this region?'

'As for saying that he was a wicked man, this was not a wicked man. The Rest Home for the Elderly of Criquebec, on the plateau. You must have heard them speaking of it? Well, the buildings came from Jaufre. He gave them to the town. He understood business!'

On the Square not one girl. The thought of the dead old man with this ghastly wound to the neck was terrifying them.

On the other hand, there were several urchins, excited by the presence of the inspector. They said 'The Detective.' And of course they played at detectives and gangsters. Every five minutes one or the other shouted in a shrill voice:

'Hands up! Hands up or I fire!' This had the benefit of making the sleeping village policeman mounting guard start up from his chair on the threshold of Jaufre's dark house.

Other urchins were making the joke faeces, bought at the *Wish to Please*, work on the boundary stone. Others were letting off cap pistols and lighting crackers, also bought at Miss Beluge's place.

'Hands up! Hands up!'

Aubin sat up, half turning: 'Come a little closer, rascals, and I'll break your backs! I'll bust your snouts I will! Bust your noses … .'

At the widow Angat's house tea was steaming in the cups. The old ladies were nervous; the thought of the crime preoccupied all of them. The signs of weariness on Clémence's face were becoming marked more quickly than on other days, and Amandine's leaden face brightened up less quickly. They did not hear the bursts of laughter which usually escaped from Zélie. Vasseur and Frelasset were also very troubled. Only the widow remained in her seat.

'What do you think of this tragedy, Mr. Lepicq?'

'My goodness, Madam, it would be premature ... . All the same I'm given to understand that Farjoux inclines towards the theory of a foul murder. The eight hundred francs which have disappeared ... .'

'But – according to you?'

'How would I have an opinion? It's possible that theft has been the motive. On the other hand, revenge ... .'

Lepicq was becoming a Norman!

'Jaufre's past is little enough known. What associations did he have at Havre? It's true you'll tell me that after ten years ... .'

'A little milk, Mr. Lepicq?'

'A drop, with pleasure.'

'A petit four?'

One or other of these women occasionally turned a furtive glance towards the door of the Uranus room. Everyone was thinking of it. But ... . Making the table turn today, that was not possible! Jaufre was occupying the core of their worries, this death was really far too recent! It had been a sacrilege to appeal so soon to a soul that had perhaps still not had the will to detach itself firmly from that flesh that it had animated for so long. In the obscurity and silence of the fusty bedroom, perhaps Jaufre's lonely spirit was watching over the body of Jaufre? Because there was nobody at the bedside of the deceased. Not a parent, not a friend, no sympathetic figure. They had left him all alone, as when he was alive. Had they thought of lighting a couple of candles, of putting a little holy water in a saucer, a sprig of boxwood? After all Jaufre was a Christian!.

'Lord,' Clémence Maisondieu suddenly cried out, very pale. 'Someone has tipped something into my tea!'

'But no, come my dear Clémence!'

'I'm certain of it! It has an odd taste.'

'Anyway, it's the same as the tea we're drinking!'

'I tell you that they have put something in my tea. First of all it's darker, that's obvious. Ah, my dream told me! They are seeking to poison me.'

'You're mad!' Amandine groaned.

Clémence was standing up, wild-eyed.

'It's burning me! My head's spinning. I can't see clearly any more!'

Indeed, her face was in a sweat, her legs giving way.

'When you have finished your play-acting!' Amandine burst out aggressively.

The women bustled around, rallying, supporting Clémence, but not fretting unduly. Clémence Maisondieu saw microbes and poison everywhere. This fixed idea – disease! She ended up by feeling the symptoms she imagined.

'Come, my dear Clémence, what do you want. It will be your liver!'

Hands on hips, Noémi regarded the old girl with scorn.

'Sit down,' the widow said. 'There … . There … . You feel better already, I'm sure of it! Now, watch! I'm drinking it, your tea! Well, it has the taste of everyone else's!'

'I found it bitter,' said Clémence, who was calming down. 'I will have carelessly put in only one sugar!'

A weak smile arose on her lips.

'Last night I dreamed of the end of the world.'

'It's the end of the world every day for someone,' Amandine threw in, shrugging her shoulders. 'When one has a life line like you have the chance of having a … .'

'And not only that!' The widow insisted. 'I recall very well having drawn your psychopredictive likeness. The Sun in House I (the House of Health) and Jupiter at the door … . You have your little worries, but deep down, you are as solid as a bridge!'

Clémence was all smiles. Her stomach pains were becoming quieter and dispersing.

'You must be finding me quite mad!'

Lepicq had witnessed the scene impassively. He

wondered for a moment why the atmosphere, the mood, seemed different from the previous evening. The murder? ... . No! It was not because of the murder. Something – which was missing ... .

Fernande Vassel wanted to know Lepicq's opinion on the matter of the code drawn by Jaufre on the postcard. The lawyer spoke of siding with the argument of the police – that these codes had no relationship with the murder. Jaufre was doing his accounts. Of no interest!

The front door slammed. They heard running in the hall. Noémi erupted breathless into the salon.

'That's it! The police officer has not been long!'

'He arrested someone?'

'Barnaby! He was the murderer. I know it from Aubin.'

'You see, Angèle!' Zélie said. 'You were mocking my method!'

'*Aragoni Labilasse Eptalicon* ... . The first paper which reappears on the water, that's the favoured one! And the first paper carried the mute's name!'

'Barnaby has confessed?' Lepicq asked.

'What do you think? He puts his neck out of joint to make a sign that it isn't him! Only ... .'

'Farjoux has proof?'

'You're joking! Eight bank notes. He recovered them again from the mute's mattress! As a hiding place it was a bit naive!'

'That inspector did not seem to me very able,' said the widow. 'I was mistaken! He knows his onions.'

'Under these conditions,' Vasseur declared, 'there is no longer reason to forbid entry to Jaufre's house. It's improper to leave it any longer without anyone to watch and pray. I suggest that we ... .'

'I'm ready to go there,' the widow and the butcher's wife spoke together.

'Me too,' said Amandine Maisondieu in her masculine voice.

'I won't go,' murmured Clémence, pallid. 'Me, the dead
… '

She had no need to mention it! They expected it!

'Me, I'll go,' said Zélie Beluge, in a brave but slightly
trembling voice.

★ ★ ★

'Hands up! Hands up or I fire!' The urchins cried on
the sun-drenched Square.

Lepicq smiled. He was finally coming to understand
what made this day so different from yesterday. This
clamouring of kids! These 'Hands up or I fire! Surrender,
you're nicked! In the name of the law I arrest you!' And
these crackers! These cap pistols! This aggressive hullaballoo!
Normally the youngsters rarely appeared on the Square, too
quiet for them. They preferred to rush like demons through
the alleys of Middle or Upper Criquebec, or give
themselves over to wild horseracing on the Plateau. Their
shrieks, that's what was a novelty on the Square. And what
was missing was the gentle presence of young girls, driven
away by the odious notions of murder, of the police, which
by contrast had attracted the urchins. What was missing was
the magical, light-hearted song '*Am Stram Gram, Femina
Godam, Carabim Zigolo ….*' There were the recitals of Ball at
the Wall '*One foot. Other foot. Still. Don't laugh. In front.
Behind. Behind in front.*' And the exasperating incantation of
little Bladout '*Bluewhitered … Bluewhitered ….*'

'Excuse me ladies,' said Lepicq. 'I must go and
congratulate the inspector.'

CHAPTER 8

OUR FRIEND DEATH

'This wing is reserved for women. The men occupy Ward B. The common room… .'

Lecorbin was doing the honours at the Old People's Rest Home.

'Admirable!' The forensic pathologist exclaimed repeatedly.

'Marvellous!' The magistrate outmatched this.

The clerk of the court appeared to have lost his tongue; he simulated the mute, swinging his head.

'Our state of the art refectory … .'

Brot the concierge, led the company. He was carrying an enormous bunch of keys which he made jangle in the manner of an altar server accompanying a priest giving the last sacraments.

Inspector Farjoux, his mind in Rouen, followed without enthusiasm. He was thinking of his wife. This evening he would be near her. From now on he had to hope that nothing would happen. He smiled. This Jaufre affair had been conducted briskly. A puzzle for a novice!

Lepicq went out onto the courtyard. He was streaming with sweat. They had taken him first to the prison. Surely he would find Farjoux there … . But there: 'Farjoux has just left,' he had been told. 'He took himself off to Pibole's place … .' Down to Pibole's place. The inspector had actually come to make a telephone call to Rouen – then he had left again. He was going up to Mr. Lecorbin. Lepicq had arrived at Lecorbin's home – a large and beautiful house decorated richly with cascading wistaria. No luck, the mayor with his gentlemen had just left for the Town Hall. Lepicq dashed to the Town Hall but arrived there to learn that these gentlemen were on their way to the Rest Home.

Eventually he caught them up!

'Bah!' said the inspector who was a modest man; this was hardly witchcraft! Barnaby hadn't a shilling; he recognised the habits of old people ... .

'The astonishing thing,' Lepicq slipped in, 'is that he had taken so long to make up his mind to carry out his wicked act. Consider that he has always been penniless! And there were ten years during which he was acquainted with the habits of the elderly!'

'The temptation to end up by being on top. And then, it had perhaps come to him from needs we don't know. A woman goes by ...'

'In any case, you've got your hands on the notes quickly!'

'Even so, he was hardly a wizard! In the mattress! The mute hadn't much imagination!'

That was exactly what was bothering Lepicq. Extreme naivety, excessive lack of shrewdness ... . He could not help telling himself that if a mattress is the first hiding place which comes to the mind of a simpleton, it is also that which a wily murderer will pick ... wishing suspicion to fall on an innocent! Someone kills Jaufre for a secret reason. He takes the eight hundred francs to create the belief of a theft. He goes to hide this money in the house of a disabled person, poor, disliked, regarded as wicked, who was the sole intimate of the old man. The notes are concealed in the mattress. If the police don't find them all will be lost! All the same, Lepicq kept these thoughts to himself.

'So that the postcard ... .'

'Precisely what one thought; irrelevant.'

'Could I see it?'

The inspector handed it to him

'We are going on to the Refectory,' said Lecorbin. 'After you Judge; after you Doctor … .'

'But … where the devil are they, your old folk?' The Doctor wondered. 'Have they run away?'

'Well, the thing is … .' Lecorbin said, embarrassed. 'We … We have no-one at the moment.'

'Bravo!' The judge spoke. 'No needy in Criquebec! There's a really model village! That gives a high opinion of its administration! Compliments, Mayor!'

'We do what we can! The great struggle against misery … . Misfortune always comes quickly enough! In any case, we await resolutely those whom adversity will strike!'

Lepicq had remained alone in the vast yard of the Hospice. His mind's eye was wandering over the numerals written by Jaufre. He heard, as through a dream, fragments of Lecorbin's brassy voice:

'Your opinion, judge – frankly? This refectory … . Do you think these poor old people will be all right?'

'Pampered like gods! You are an organiser, my dear Mr. Lecorbin! A driving force!'

'Pooh! Pooh! … .' Said the Mayor, who was drinking milk. At the back of Lepicq's memory, the small girls were singing. '*Am Stram Gram, Femina Godam* … .' And Bladout's youngest daughter, who did not put a space between the words: '*Bleublanrouge … bleublanrouge* … .'

It was to these three words, arbitrarily linked, that Lepicq owed making a discovery whose exceptional fundamental importance, however, was to appear to him only much later.

Jaufre's postcard was the opposite of Bluewhitered!

Lepicq crossed the refectory at the double, climbed the steps leading to the women's dormitory and caught the inspector on the threshold.

'One second, can you? I've just come to make a comment! These numbers written by Jaufre … .'

'Well?'

'They're not numbers!'

'What?'

Lepicq took out a pencil and, between each group of two numerals, traced a dotted line.

'Confound it!' Farjoux gawped. 'That's amazing!'

The numerals had become letters. Capital letters. Whereas little Bladout had not marked the space between the words, Jaufre had imagined, on the contrary, of putting a space in the middle of the letters where normally one would not leave one. Each group of two 'numbers' was in fact only a capital letter cut vertically.

BARNAB

'Barnaby' Farjoux cried. 'The old man was not dead immediately. When the mute took his wallet, he was recognised. And he tried to tell us the ... . But no! That's ridiculous!'

'If Jaufre had wanted to expose the guilty party, he would have written the name in normal legible writing. He would not have amused himself in calligrapic fancies, aiming to put letters for numbers! One had to concede that the old figure had given himself over to this weird cryptographic exercise before the murder, when he did not suspect the presence of the mute behind the heavy curtains. And it was the knife attack which had prevented him from transforming the last Y of Barnaby into numerals.'

'With what intention ? ... .'

'Right! With what intention?'

'That is perhaps only further proof against the mute, if that has significance!' The inspector concluded.

Lepicq remained silent. He was reflecting on the two men whose embarrassed attitude had intrigued him at the murder scene. Genêtou and Doré, the hearty fellows with the briefcases ... . Was it really Jaufre who had drawn the disguised letters on the card? This card, had it not been brought rather by the clerk or the secretary and slipped under the corpse? The lawyer made an effort to recollect the detail of the scenes which had taken place in the gloomy dump, the positions occupied by the people present, their comings and goings, their actions. Neither Doré nor Genêtou had touched the body.

Only Dr. Pouacre ... .

For Farjoux it was all simple. Barnaby had delivered the blow. They held the guilty man and the proof. The matter was settled. And he, Farjoux, would be at his wife's bedside that evening.

Lepicq left the Home. He was tempted to position himself close to Barnaby, then decided against it. What was the point? He set off down the slope.

Strange town Criquebec! At the lower end wealth. And the higher one went, the more the fortunes of the citizens declined. So that, leaving behind the large incomes, the well-to-do buildings, the influential businesses, one came to affluence, to middle-class houses still very comfortable, to businesses still prosperous, then came the modest private means, the sales and shops which supported the low incomes, earning little but making up in quantity! The level of the hard working, the beavers; one penny on another penny counts.

Going on up, one came across the employed, the workers, all those who subsist from just single means which brings meanly-paid unrewarding labour. After that, there were the homes where they did not eat meat every day, where they paid attention to the paraffin, where they bunched together in a tight semi-circle facing the low-heat fireplace. The ones who had never had any luck – or who had had it, but had lacked foresight. Right at the top, slum houses, corrugated iron and tarred paper, nests for crows; it rained into the lofts, the wind put its mouth to the broken tiles and froze one's buttocks under the horse blanket. They didn't eat meat or vegetables twice a day, they made wine with a litre of vinegar and 100 ml. of water, they used eyes for a candle, they burned dead wood full of smoke. There, God knows how they were, for only 800 hundred francs ....

Lepicq did not feel at all in a mood to enquire. Behind the curtains, all these profiles of the elderly ... Getting involved? Putting crafty questions? Collecting a ragbag of gossip, tittle-tattle, insinuations, slanders, libels, observing that people here, like everywhere else, took less pleasure from a stroke of luck which came to them from here or there, than from the annoyances which came to others? Time lost!

Lepicq went down towards the Square without haste.

In Criquebec they practiced the policy of compensations.

Those on the heights starved but they had good air and a healthy wind. Whereas the moneybags down below lived with dust in summer and microbes in winter. A gilded dust it's true, and luxurious microbes, but dust and microbes all the same! ... .

On the actual Square, there were no great fortunes. Frelasset ran his business, but he was not putting his million aside every year! A hundred banknotes at the most. Beluge, Vasseur, Médéric Plainchant managed – no more. The widow Angat had means but they did not stretch very far. The Maisondieus maintained their position but from out of three pennyworth of income they wouldn't have to stray too far. On the Square, it was better than large fortunes, these were the old families of the town, the line of pioneers; the nobility of Criquebec. As in America, there are those who had at the time someone on the famous Mayflower.

Lepicq went down quietly.

All round they were talking of the Incident. There were many who, timidly feeling pity for Jaufre's fate, were revising their judgement on him.

They had it in for him because of this Hospice; they were not perhaps altogether right. It was not Jaufre's fault that the indigents preferred begging, living on crusts, dressing in rags, sleeping on pallets rather than going up to the Rest Home on the pretext that they held on to their independence, and their dignity! Their dignity! They put it oddly! Stubborn, yes! ... . There had been this question of revenue, the eight hundred francs, which could go down badly. Ah well, didn't Jaufre have the right to live? The town had owed him 96,000 francs. Right. But if they wanted to do sums ... . The buildings and outbuildings on the plateau were easily worth two hundred thousand. So the town benefited by 100,000 all round. There are much worse speculations!

And one could look far before finding a Rest Home which could compare itself to that in Criquebec. It was admirable! Yes, perhaps they had been a little unfair to Jaufre... .

When Lepicq arrived on the Square, women were going into the dead man's house with a meditative air.

They were watching over the dead man. Widow Angat had brought beautiful cotton sheets. They had carried out the last washing with care. Zélie had provided two candles, Vasseur also. And they prayed. They pampered Jaufre – if one can say it. He had had so little of it while he was alive. They were remembering. Each month he took himself to Gratoulet's house. It wasn't far but he could scarcely hold himself up! They saw him again, in his old yellow jacket, his pathetic trousers, his poverty-stricken seediness, his shoes which had lost their heels ... . How pitiful! Could not the tax man have spared him this trip, sending his assistant – a young lad who would scarcely have worn out his legs carrying eight hundred francs and the register for signature?

These hypocritical comments were passed without affectation. The women cast distressed looks over the miserable furniture, the damp flaking walls, the broken floorboards and the overall disorder, the total abandon of this pitiful home! Poor old man, without anyone to give a thought to his housekeeping, to his old rags, to his eating … . And this rascal Barnaby, who was biding his time! Had people so little heart! Anyway … . The interment would be at the town's expense. They must hope that the municipality would make appropriate arrangements. That was really the least … . They would have the whole world at the ceremony. If Jaufre saw that from up there it would delight him.

The hotel Pibole swarmed with customers. The terrace was packed. A telegram was waiting for Lepicq, sent by Jugonde the lawyer's young secretary.

'You indicated affair of stolen jewellery rue Juliette Dodu and affair of anonymous letters containing death threats addressed to grocer rue Portefoin. Planning to follow up? Good holiday.'

On a page from a notebook Lepicq composed this reply:

'Good holiday jewel thefts! Long life grocer! I stay at Criquebec. Wish you happy love affairs!'

On the pavement, the Pibole's child was uttering ferociously the war cry of the Stranglers of the Far West. Lepicq grabbed him by the scruff of the neck and passed a ten franc piece under his nose:

'Run and take this telegram to the post, little one! With what I'm giving you, you can buy a buffalo gun!'

On the terrace, the lawyer caught sight of two figures of his acquaintance, Doré and Genêtou. They smiled at him half rising. There was something servile in their manner.

'Well then,' Lepicq said. 'This murder?'

'The inspector is able!' Genêtou offered meaningfully.

'Very able!' The lawyer concurred. His nearly closed

velvet eyelids let slip only a fleeting glance.

They kept to trivial comments. Lepicq was fanning himself with the postcard on which Jaufre, or someone else, had written *Barnab* in capital letters disguised as numbers.

Lepicq had adopted more than usually his air of door-to-door crimes salesman: 'I am Mr. Lepicq, well-known on the Paris market-place' he seemed to be saying. 'Lepicq, the man who puts juries in his pocket! Fees for all purses; prices according to client's means – and no mistake about that! The total amount of the fee does not affect the quality of the speech for the defence. We always provide superior products, the best quality in eloquence. A word to the wise is enough! Think about it. Don't rush. I have plenty of time.'

'Another drink?' Genêtou proposed.

'Well!' Lepicq said 'It's only the last one that kills!'

The dwarf Couril was pacing aggressively up and down the Square. People were sniggering. The dwarf raised his head and stared at them, as though in defiance.

★ ★ ★

That evening after dinner Lepicq took himself off to loiter under Reine Coulemelle's window. A lamp was burning. The shadow of the post office employee stood out against the flowered paper. The woman was holding a cup which she raised to her lips. Some infusion ... She had just finished her meal.

Not a soul on the Patte-d'Oie-du-Petit-Roi.

Reine Coulemelle opened her glass-fronted wardrobe, took from it dresses and hats which she laid on the bed.

'Perfect,' Lepicq said to himself. 'She's going out. This time I'll know where she takes herself.'

Reine Coulemelle removed her skirt. She did not immediately go over to the dress that she had got ready to put on. She prepared herself first: ironing, rouge on cheeks, lipstick, powder. Then she tried a hat, rejected it and tried another; that one would do. She slipped into a dress of floral print material. Yet again ran a comb through her hair. Lepicq, like a lover, grew impatient. 'God! What a time! ... . What a time!' As if he didn't know that all women take a time!

He went to take up a position in a corner. From there he watched the two possible exits which Reine Coulemelle might take; that of the rue du Pot-de-Grès and that of the Étourneaux. The night was sultry and stormy. The muggy gloom stuck to the skin, pressed on the head, the face, confined it like a balaclava hat, fitting the body like a jersey on a cat burglar.

Lepicq refained from smoking; the glow of a cigarette would have given him away.

Reine Coulemelle blew out her lamp. The lawyer's glances started to switch from the rue du Pots-de-Grès to the rue des Étourneaux. Again a long spell on lookout.

What was she up to?

Waiting. And suddenly:

'Heck! That's it then!'... . Reine Coulemelle went back to her room and put the light on. In front of the mirror, she removed her hat and took off her floral dress. She had finished her trip. And she had not left either by the rue du Pot-de-Grès or by the rue des Étourneaux.

'I'm diddled! There's a third way out!'

Her time away had scarcely been more than twenty minutes. Coulemelle had not been able to go far.

The lawyer withdrew, furious. Abruptly he slowed down his step.

Someone ... .

No reason to look twice; the walker had the height of a ten-year-old child. But children of ten years were in bed at this time. It was Couril. He too was interested in the clandestine trips of Reine Coulemelle!

'Good evening sir,' said Lepicq, raising his hat.

'Good night, sir!' replied the quiet and ill-mannered

little man, in a voice so soft and gentle that the lawyer, brought up short, distanced himself without taking advantage of this unusual occasion for engaging in conversation.

When he found himself in the Square, the light was shining above the *Wish to Please* shop, in Zélie Beluge's dining room. Médéric Plainchant was neither in his shop nor his flat. The lawyer saw him in Pibole's; he was playing dominoes with Gratoulet and the Gentil couple.

Lepicq then carried out a mad act. He didn't think. Impetuously he gave in to impulse.

On the right of the *Good Swordsman* shop, there was a coach door. It wasn't locked. Discreetly, the lawyer pushed. To the left, under the arch, a stairway began. Lepicq climbed it. He stopped on the first landing, in front of door of the cutler's flat. This door was locked, but scruples did not embarrass Lepicq. He picked the lock. From Plainchant's room he saw Zélie. She was asleep over a paper.

Lepicq found all he wanted on a pedestal table; a lamp, sheets of thick paper, and a charcoal pencil. He lit the lamp. Immediately, Zélie turned her head in his direction. Lepicq was bent over. She must have believed that she was dealing with Plainchant. In large figures he wrote a number, the first that came to mind: 46. He raised the sheet and the lamp. Zélie read the number, leafed through a small notebook (the secret code), and began to laugh!

In turn she wrote a number: 182.

'Now I'm doing well!' The lawyer said to himself. 'This conversation in the dark can go on for a long time!'

He wrote another number, the same as before but reversed: 64.

Zélie's expression changed, she became irritated. She began to write. This time, Lepicq decoded, no longer a number but letters. Zélie had written 'Insolent fellow! You've been drinking! Go and lie down!' Thereupon, shrugging her shoulders, she slammed the shutters furiously.

'Gosh! What have I been able to transmit to her that's so shocking?'

He looked for the copy of the secret code that Plainchant had to have. He didn't find it and withdrew.

'The cutler is going to get a proper dressing down tomorrow! With all that, he will know that someone has had the nerve to force an entry into his home.'

He half-opened the carriage doorway cautiously and risked a look; the path appeared clear and he put a cautious foot onto the Square. Immediately, he jumped: 'Nabbed.'

'Good evening, sir!' A soft voice whispered.

Francis Couril raised his hat, smiling graciously.

'Good night, sir,' replied Prosper Lepicq blandly.

★ ★ ★

Jaufre's funeral was held two days later, a Sunday, at the town's expense. It was a beautiful interment. Rich decoration at the home of the departed, as in the church where they put up a superb catafalque. The coffin was of solid oak with silver handles. Really very good. A sung service. Plenty of flowers (Zélie, who was well up on this subject, had assisted the florist). Several top quality wreaths. The one from the Town Council was mentioned – impressive. Frankly very, very good. A considerable crowd followed the funeral procession. More accurately, the whole of Criquebec. The town was emptied. There remained left scarcely more than the too small and the too old – The latter looking after the former, unless it was the other way round!.

The cemetery was on the eastern part of the plateau opposite the Hospice. The climb was slow, stately and contemplative.

As they arrived at the summit from the side, row upon row of the people turned around. They were unable to do otherwise; it was stronger than they were. The lure of the

76

vastness, the temptation of allowing one's gaze to plummet from the summit over the town. Right at the bottom the Square shone white, like a plate. On its surface a small black silhouette moved; the dwarf Couril was executing his eternal pacing up and down! Really, that being wasn't human!

Following final prayers the Mayor, to general surprise, improvised a speech over the grave. Brief, tactful and furthermore quite heartfelt. They were a little astonished at first to hear him on affectionate terms with the deceased, but on consideration told themselves it was more respectful.

Jaufre, we have come, all your friends. We were anxious to accompany you to your resting place, to make our farewell to you. This is not a family in mourning that you are leaving, Jaufre. It is more than a family – a town in mourning! Emotion grips me – I want to say just a few words.

I know. Wicked tongues, which spare no-one, have not spared you, not even you! They have spread slanders on your account. But we are decided on what has been, and that you have had a life without a stain, of honour, dignity, study. You were a character, an independent man. It is because of this you did not hesitate to leave a brilliant post in the Registration Department – an act which many in your place would have thought twice about before doing, on account of the pension which was there at the end! You, you put liberty above all!

But, when the time came you had no more than one thought: Criquebec, the town which had seen your birth … . You returned, modestly, to end your days there where they had begun, there where you had tasted the first joys of childhood. You worked, you meditated, they knew it and respected your solitude.

Jaufre, I can certainly detect in you the badge of a charitable man. None of your friends present here will contradict me. You are the dead victim of your charity. You gave a portion of your meagre resources to an unworthy individual, you nursed a serpent in your bosom, and worse than a serpent, for beasts kill only to defend or

77

nourish themselves! You were killed by a man who sponged off you! But the murderer will be punished, justice will prevail!

I have finished, Jaufre. A last word and I have finished .... I come to award you the badge of a charitable man. Before saluting you one last time I would like to give you another title – perhaps a finer one. That of Benefactor of your Town! Thanks to you Jaufre, thanks to your generosity, there arises on this plateau a House welcoming all the needy, all the poor, all those stricken badly, to all those whom age makes powerless. I wish to speak of our wonderful Retirement Home.

On this matter, I am the bearer of a piece of good news. If only I had had the pleasure of being able to announce it to you in your lifetime! But, from where you are, you are hearing me! ... .'

Lecorbin made a practised pause. From his jacket pocket, he pulled out his glasses, whose lenses he wiped on a handkerchief. Then he unfolded a piece of paper:

'Yesterday, three poor old persons from Criquebec put in a request to the Town Hall for admission to the Retirement Home. This morning, we recorded two other requests. ... .'

He refolded the paper.

'To all these requests, a favorable reply will be made. These five compatriots that poverty and illness are going to take to the House of Refuge, it is in your name, Jaufre, that they will be welcomed! And it is in their name that I say to you – Thanks! You have deserved Criquebec! Farewell, dear fellow citizen! Goodbye, dear comrade! Rest in peace!'

'Monumental!' Prosper Lepicq reflected.

The valedictory had an effect. The women were weeping. Many of the men regretted that it was not the custom to applaud in cemeteries, for the words of Lecorbin were worthy of loud approbation ... .

And the best part is that the women who were weeping were truly afflicted, all touched and and softened at the thought of the old man who was taken off! This old man whom everyone had held in contempt, cursed, execrated, accused of misappropriation of funds, whose

78

passing gave rise to sniggers and insults, whom they had left to die in the gutter, to whom they summoned death each morning and evening!

'However it's true,' in tears the women told themselves. 'He liked his own company.' And the men; 'It's true, he did a great deal for his town.'

By virtue of the assassin's knife and the mayor's eloquence Jaufre, the Exploiter of Criquebec, had become its Benefactor!

Incidentally, someone who had not wasted his time on the freshly dug funeral mound, was Lecorbin! He had come simply to assure his election at the next change of the Regional Council, which was to take place in six weeks!

CHAPTER 9

THE WOMANISER

Those old ladies were feeling confused.

Jaufre had now rested in the cemetery for five days.

The *Yvetot Gazette* had just arrived. The widow had scarcely taken off the wrapping before Frelasset, pointing an index finger:

'Look at that then!' ... . She indicated the following advertisement:

HUMANITARIAN OFFER TO ALL THOSE WHO
SUFFER,
TO ALL THOSE WHO DOUBT,
TO ALL THOSE WHO DESPAIR.

Do you wish to triumph?
Do you wish to succeed?

PROFESSOR ALFA,
Member of the Academy of Occult Sciences,
Founder of the Scandinavian Psycho-Analytical Institute,
Medium Authorised by the Learned.

After long years of study and observation on the spot, the most
astonishing secrets have been extracted from the Far North.
Mysteries of the Past and of the Future unveiled by a completely
new method. Magic Snow. Magnetic Irradiation. Northern-Lights
Horoscope. The Arctic Circle. The Antartic Circle. The Human
Being, like the Stars, has its poles, its negative and positive

electricity, its magnetic explosions. Is it not obvious how two and two make four?

PROFESSOR ALFA *will reveal to you the Key for the development of Interior Forces. Possessing the Knowledge, you will have the Power at your disposal. To convince you, a personal study will be sent to you free, without obligation on your part. Send your name and first name (Mr., Mrs. or Miss) in your own handwriting together with your place and date of birth (the exact hour if possible). You can include two francs in stamps, if you wish, for correspondence expenses.*

Address the correspondence to PROFESSOR ALFA, Department 418, Service R.T., 169, boulevard Saint-Germain, Paris.

HAPPINESS. BUSINESS. LOVE. WEALTH. HEALTH.

PROFESSOR ALFA does not make personal appearances.

This text was framed with a stylised effigy of an enigmatic figure with a fur hat on in place of the traditional fakir's turban. A huge sun, which could only be the Midnight Sun, gave him a halo and from the four cardinal points rays laden with impulses.

In the kitchen, Noémi was laughing like a lunatic. The widow Frelasset had taken herself to Havre. Nothing unfortunate had resulted from this trip, despite the warning given by the Hatpins – 'Renounce a dangerous journey.' Frelasset had brought back to Noémi, on the latter's request, a 'Letter of Good Fortune' which she had bought for ten sous, from a disabled person in the port. This letter was the cause of the servant's hilarity.

To brighten the Heavens, God created the Birds. But, because of their speed, he used them as messengers. They carry his Commandments from Planet to Planet, and Star to Star. Sometimes they come to land on Earth and carry to certain people the secret of their existence. You have a great regard for your character. It's true that it's perfect. You incline towards the ill-favoured. Carry on. God sees everything from the height of his blue Heaven and will reward you. But do not regard as a negligible quantity the nature of people in your family circle. Under uncouth exteriors, some may hide noble spirits. Thus, in your family, there is one of your kin that seems to you discredited. You are wrong. He will become celebrated and you will benefit from his good fortune. Moreover, you yourself will achieve glory through your merit, and love will crown your efforts. But struggle against a major fault; renounce playing the horses. You will visit Switzerland, Canada and Persia. In this last country you will get yourself married.

Can you imagine anything more ridiculous? This relative who could become famous (Noémi no longer had anyone)! Noémi achieving celebrity status! Noémi playing the horses! Noémi, who had never put her feet outside her Normandy, visiting Switzerland, Canada, Persia, and taking a husband in this last country! … .

Intrigued by the exclamations of the women, the servant went through to the living room, with a scornful smile on her lips from Professor Alfa's advertisement.

'Another charlatan!'

'On the other hand perhaps he is a great scholar,' Vasseur protested.

'I'm telling you he's a shyster! A swindler of gullible brains! These people make themselves fat on the backs of simpletons!'

They shrugged their shoulders. Noémi was a sceptic. What good discussing it?

At that moment Clémence Maisondieu arrived.

'I slept well last night,' she said! 'I have only had two nightmares. A dream of candles that one blew out, and another where I saw myself shut away in a cellar. In principle this is a bad sign, but the interment of Mr. Jaufre explains everything. The candles, they were the candles at the church; and the cellar was the tomb at the cemetery.'

'Surely,' said Zélie, 'be that as it may, if only you would follow my recipe, you would have only pleasant dreams, just like me!'

'What do you dream about incidentally?'

'Birds, butterflies, lakes! I wander by boat. Often, I see flowers, I gather them, I make bouquets.'

Touching Zélie, who had preserved the youthfulness of the heart! Lepicq contemplated this Ophélia with white hair.

'Or better, I'm flying … .'

'You're flying?'

'Yes. I'm running, I'm feeling light, and that's it; I'm floating. I'm taking flight, I'm passing over hills, woods, and I'm off; I'm going a long way, but a long way! … . Sometimes, I put myself down on the other side of Yvetot! It's pleasant! Just thinking of it, I pine for my bed! One should never wake up!'

'Speak for yourself!' Clémence replied. 'But tell me, how do you land? Do you perform like aeroplanes, or swoop down right on to the ground?'

'I come whirling down, rather like a leaf!'

'Ah well, I wouldn't want to frighten you, my dear Beluge but, in your place I would be wary. Flying is not as good as that. You should consult Dr. Pouacre, so that he can look at your heart.'

'My heart? I wouldn't change my heart for all the gold in the world!' said Zélie.

'And the numbers, Miss?' Lepicq said. 'Do they come to you when dreaming?'

'Never!' said Zélie, with a suspicious look.

The day following the evening when Lepicq had introduced himself into Plainchant's place, Beluge had had a stormy discussion on the subject of number 64, the cheeky coded message.

'Not possible, dear friend,' Plainchant was ironic, 'you

are becoming a sleepwalker! I didn't send you numbers that evening! I was playing dominoes at Pibole's!'

'Yes! And you drank to the point of no longer remembering what you did afterwards! It's a disgrace!'

'Not at all! You were dreaming!'

'Not at all! You were drunk!'

Now Zélie was sleeping on the evening in question. And Plainchant, who never drank, had taken a little extra. Uncertain, they had considered the incident as closed. But that had left them puzzled.

The boy from Pibole brought a telegram for Lepicq.

'You point out improper solicitation of Bezon legacy. There would have been a deceased suspect. Case seems interesting. Busy gathering documentation that will be sent you soonest. Wish you a good stay Criquebec. Devoted regards. Jugonde.'

Lepicq made an irritated gesture.

'My secretary persecutes me!'

'Don't complain,' the widow said. 'For each one who has too much conscience, there are ninety-nine who are lacking it!'

She pointed her podgy index finger towards the window, drawing back the curtain.

'Hullo! He's back!'

'Who then?'

'The police inspector. It was to be expected!'

Expected, yes indeed. Barnaby, whom they had taken to Yvetot, continued to deny like the very devil. Moreover, the judge had received some twenty anonymous letters. The name of Couril the dwarf figured a great deal in this correspondence written *to render a service to Justice*, and signed *A friend of the Truth. (You will understand that I have no wish to cause trouble by signing my name!)*

The night in Criquebec passed oddly. On the nature of this oddness, the men and women were in disagreement.

But everyone was certain that the dwarf was at the bottom of these disturbances.

According to the men, Couril was a womaniser, a cynical Don Juan. Their wives protested. 'That midget? That freak? Handsome seducer!'

'Exactly!' The men replied. His ugliness, his deformity; such were the dwarf's trump cards. Honest women, who would have rejected the advances of a normal individual, let themselves be led on by an unwholesome curiosity. They yielded to the attraction which *monstrosity* exercises on the imagination. On the other hand, the women maintained that Couril corrupted their husbands. In Criquebec, with the involvement of certain shameless characters, like the Coulemelle woman, not to name her, orgies and seances were organised in which the dwarf was the prime mover. Couril set up the clandestine diversions of Criquebec!

Don Juan or the evil genius, never, it's true, caught in the act. But – returning to the crime – perhaps Jaufre had uncovered something serious; serious enough to push a man to murder … . Where was Couril at the time of the killing?

The examining magistrate was a sufficiently decent man to prefer even parcels of excrement to these poisonous messages in a disguised hand on standard paper. Nevertheless, he had made Farjoux return from Rouen.

'I would like you to pop down there, inspector. Shake up this dwarf for me, so that we can see what he has on his mind!'

Couril was pacing up and down the Square. The policeman headed straight for him.

'I have some questions to put to you, Mr. Couril.'

'At your service, Mr. Inspector.'

They went off towards the Town Hall. Lepicq caught them up in the rue de l'Eglise.

The inspector shook his hand cordially. He had conceived some respect for Lepicq, since that demonstration of the dots which converted numbers into letters.

'Still nothing, you know!' he said. 'It isn't natural! Whatever the doctor says, I'm anxious.'

He was speaking of his wife, who was still awaiting her child.

Lepicq took him aside.

'It would interest me to be present at the interrogation. I would like to know your technique. But I'm fearful of being intrusive!'

'You must be joking!' Farjoux exclaimed. 'I'll be delighted. In a sense, you're one of us. There'll be two studying his reactions. Afterwards, we'll have an apéritif.'

'You'll lunch with me, I hope?'

'With pleasure. We'll chat. Two heads are better than one!'

From the way in which Farjoux launched into the interrogation, it was clear that he had not studied the Socratic method, otherwise called the *art of revealing minds*, at the same school as Lepicq!

'It happens like that in Criquebec!'

The dwarf regarded him vaguely, then began to study his finger nails. His chubby hands were well-groomed; as was the rest of him for that matter. Hair cut short, clean cheeks which seemed forever to be leaving the barber's shop, perfect teeth; a good smell of cleanliness. A well-cut grey salt and pepper suit – grey increased height – dark red tie and shoes with raised heels polished to perfection.

'You go after women! … '

' Who d'you mean?' the dwarf said, fiddling with the gold chain which crossed his stomach.

He had spoken in his normal voice. For he had at his disposal three sorts of voice. That voice by which they knew him, a voice from a head perched high, relapsing into huskiness, an adolescent voice in the stage of breaking they'd said, but it never would break, Couril was forty years old! Then the voice that he ought to have, the genuine article, his serious and strong voice of a man. And a third, that he no longer ought to have, his voice from the time that he was still too small to be a dwarf, his child's voice, reedy and very sweet. Lepicq was certainly the only one in Criquebec to have heard it − when Couril, doffing his hat had said to him 'Good night, sir!'

'Who's that − running after women?' The dwarf repeated.

'Well … . You for example! It seems they pick up their little Casanova!'

The dwarf had an ambiguous look − half ironic, half secretive.

'I beg your pardon?' he said in his serious voice.

'Yes. In fact, I must tell you that we have certain information … . They report to us nocturnal scenes of abandon with which you would not be unfamiliar. You have the reputation of being a bit of a devilish womaniser, Mr. Couril! Note, as far as I am concerned, I find the business flattering! But abuse is abuse!'

To impress Lepicq with his tact, the inspector was avoiding blunt words. Lepicq was troubled to hear him say '*We* have received … . *They* report to us … .' These plurals seemed to associate him with an activity of which the mere idea greatly displeased him.

The dwarf was showing an arrogant smile!

'And then?' He said, his voice way up in the trees.

'There are complaints … .'

'Signed?'

Farjoux did not answer.

'Inspector, these complaints … .'

Now he had assumed his man's voice, rough and low-pitched. One never knew which one he was going to use. It was disconcerting!

'These complaints, I despise them! D'you believe I'm unaware? 'I turn women's heads! They can't resist me!' And when would this be? Suppose that it's so! What is the point of law which provides for this offence? I don't seduce

87

minors! I haven't even violated any young girl! How husbands defend themselves!'

He did not throw this out aggressively, but rather with quiet disdain.

'I know that's not all! I organise bacchanalias, don't I? I distract husbands from their duty! Because of me Criquebec became worse than Sodom and Gomorrha! Ah well', he concluded, 'I will register a complaint for defamation – a *signed* complaint!'

The interrogation had changed direction. Farjoux had pulled the helm over. 'After all, these affairs of petticoats don't interest me! Where were you at the moment of Jaufre's murder?'

'At the precise moment?'

'Preferably!' Farjoux groaned.

'But … you don't know it, this precise moment!'

Farjoux showed that the blow had struck home. His tone was caustic.

'Let's not play with words! Where were you on the evening of the crime, between six and eight?'

'On the Square.'

'They say not!'

'Who?'

'I'll point out to you, Mr. Couril, that it's I who puts the questions! Can you prove that you were on the Square between six and eight?'

'The proof doesn't fall to me! It's for you to provide it!'

'I advise you not to take this tone!'

'I'm no longer patient!' Couil spoke in his high voice. 'If you have a warrant, produce it!'

'But … , said Farjoux disconcerted, 'who's talking of arresting you?'

'Ah! … well!'

The policeman had not taken a good path. As for Lepicq, he guarded against opening his mouth.

'Let's suppose that I had not been on the Square,'

Couril in turn challenged. 'I'm saying that I didn't go into Jaufre's place. What's your answer?'

'Where would you have gone?'

'Without its being a large town, it's worthwhile going for a walk in Criquebec. I like to walk.'

'Along the side of Patte-d'Oie-du-Petit-Roi, for example?'

'Why not?'

'You make stops there … .'

'I haven't seen notices forbidding it!'

'What is the nature of your relation with Miss Reine Coulemelle?'

'One of pure courtesy. I greet her when I meet her. She accepts my greeting.'

Couril got up.

'We are stirring the pot! Inspector, I did not kill Jaufre. Why would I have done it? There's not a shadow of a reason, no vestige of a motive. In short, what's at the bottom of all this? These people who don't distinguish themselves with courage sent anonymous letters guaranteeing that I have dissolute morals. I answer, firstly "That remains to be proven!" Secondly "That concerns morals and not civil law!" They rely on smoke to incriminate me in the crime! Inspector, you are not from Criquebec. No more are you Mr. Lepicq. And that's so much the better for you! Ah well, listen. In Criquebec they hate me like they hated Jaufre, like they hated Barnaby! These people know only hate, petty hate! They detested Jaufre because of eight miserable hundred-franc notes per month! They loathe Barnaby because he was a poor cripple, and Jaufre's friend! Me … .'

'You?'

'Me, people hate me because I don't see at the same level as them; I'm educated, and I know how to assess them at their true value, that is, lower than the ground! Criquebec people … you know, Inspector … .'

His mouth moved. Was he going to spit on the floor?

No. He got up and moved over towards an open window, rose on to tiptoe and spat in the yard.

'There!'

Farjoux gave up pushing the interrogation further, Couril then took himself off to write his complaint, in the presence of Genêtou the mayor's secretary. His defamation against unknown persons.

CHAPTER 10

THE BLUE DRESS

In the absence of Mr. Lepicq the old ladies were assembled in the Uranus room, gathered about the round table. They had called up the spirit of Jaufre. Jaufre had not arrived. The old ladies had then attempted telepathy; that had given nothing. The widow, charged with passing on her thought, was concentrating on the notion of a sea voyage. Vasseur, charged with receiving this thought, declared 'You were reflecting on your house in Saint-Blaise.' In her turn Amandine Maisondieu concentrated, and was thinking deeply of Zélie Beluge who clearly had to gather up this psychic message. Zélie maintained 'You reflected on the case of Andréa Gauric!' Hopeless! A day lacking fluidity! For the moment Uranus must be in exile, or at loggerheads with Mercury, or frustrated by Mars. ... . These ladies were thrown back onto the *Humanitarian Offer* of Professor Alfa.

It was at that moment that Lepicq turned up.

'So?' The widow enquired. 'This interrogation?'

'No result. Couril is lying. One has to confess that they are unable to raise any charge against him.'

Zélie spoke, 'I came across a strange comment this morning. I was leafing through a glossary of magic; it's filled with amusing words. Anamalech, demon of discord, Acham, demon of Thursday; Béchet, demon of Friday ... .'

'Yes, yes ... . Well?'

'Guess what name I stumbled on? Couril!'

'Impossible!'

'As I'm telling you! And guess what a couril is in

magic? A dwarf spirit with webbed feet who haunts stones! Would you believe! ... .'

'It's incredible, that hits the nail on the head!'

'Yesterday,' Amandine spoke, 'I was able to see the inside of his left hand. His head line is cut into two sections, which indicates serious injury, madness. And I believe – I'm not certain – that these sections superimpose themselves under Saturn, which is a sign of a major fatality. This characteristic has been noticed in many criminals condemned to the guillotine.'

Lepicq, not forgetting that he had worked his way into the circle by giving physiognomy as a reference, declared that the straightforward appearance of Couril's face and cranium told him nothing of value! A flat forehead, average imagination. Thin eyebrows, moral weakness. Very deep-set eyes, a taste for espionage. Rather long, spiny nose, but thick lips and a fleshy cheek, instincts for brutality. As far as one was able to judge, his cranial protruberances revealed few tendencies towards affection and a great deal to brutality!

'What type is this astrologically?'

'A Martian cross-bred with quirkiness,' said the widow, 'Mars and the Moon linked in House X, that's to say, the Centre of Heaven – this is not brilliant! Born under Capricorn – productivity small, good eyesight.'

'And Reine Coulemelle?'

'A Venusian. She is also Capricorn.'

'That's good?'

'Yes and no. It's mitigated. Venus represents astral fluid at peace, does it not? Harmful in a feminine horoscope, it produces debauched and unprincipled women. Now, if you have the good fortune to have Jupiter or the Sun in House I ... .'

'My God! Lepicq mused. 'They'll send me mad!'

Through the window he noticed Farjoux. The inspector crossed the Square, sat himself down on the Pibole terrace after having asked: 'Nothing for me by phone?'

Lepicq deserted the women and rejoined Farjoux.

'A queer fish this dwarf!' said the inspector. 'my weakness was to have nothing definite against him. Anyway, what I make of it ... . Barnaby is the guilty one without a doubt!'

He had thrown this out without conviction, his look was seeking approval.

Lepicq tapped the inspector's knee.

'I don't believe that it's Barnaby!'

Farjoux sighed, raised his glass in which an ice cube was melting.

'All this is really a bit tricky!'

If it wasn't Barnaby, he was going to need to remain, rooted in this god-forsaken place, investigating, questioning. Whilst his wife, in Rouen ... . Not Barnaby, really? ... . All the same, the mute's guilt fitted things so well!

'You have a reason?'

'None. I simply don't believe it.'

'The dwarf then?'

'Possible. I don't know.'

The heat continued to be oppressive. They saw only faces gleaming with sweat. Most people had discarded their jackets. Few shirt collars were buttoned up. On whatever side one looked, someone was surprised in the act of mopping a forehead or temples. Only Couril, who had resumed his eternal comings and goings under the chestnuts appeared immune to the heat of the sun. Done up tightly in his salt and pepper suit, tie squeezed over his Adam's apple, he conceded nothing!

'The trouble is that if it's not the mute, there's nothing!' Farjoux exploded. 'Nothing to catch hold of! The postcard, you don't think that ... .'

Lepicq shook his head.

'The old man amused himself disguising letters as numbers. He worked on the name of Barnaby because it's the one which will have first come to mind. Barnaby was his mate.'

'This idea of turning letters into numbers!'

'A whim!'

Genêtou and Doré arrived. The lawyer made a friendly gesture to them.

Farjoux was meanwhile day-dreaming; he had an ecstatic smile.

'We'll call her Camille! He said. 'It's settled.'

'But … if it's a boy?' Lepicq said.

'We'll call him Camille all the same. That does for both. Only, my wife would prefer a girl!'

Lepicq dipped a hand into his pocket to get his cigarettes, and felt a piece of paper at the ends of his fingers.

'Hang it all! A telegram from my secretary. I had completely forgotten it!' He looked at his watch.

'Quarter to seven. The post office presumably has to shut at seven o'clock.'

'If you get a move on, you'll make it.'

'I'll find you here for dinner?'

'O.K.'

The postmistress had a pleasant expression, an absent look, as if turned inwards. In the office no other customer but Lepicq. The clock showed four minutes to seven.

'The office is going to close I believe, Miss?'

'Yes sir,' Reine Coulemelle replied. 'But a few minutes more or less … '

The voice was agreeable – gentle, remote.

Reine Coulemelle … Forty years … An old girl. Why old girl? She didn't lack charm. Subtle charm, a little subdued, a pastel shade. The voice, look, traits; all contributed towards giving this impression of retreat, of distance. Where was she, this woman? She held herself behind a counter, seemed in attendance, said 'A few minutes more or less … ' But where was she in reality? In what direction of time did her thoughts wander? Towards the past? The future?

On the terrace of the Pibole hotel Farjoux sipped his

anis. The alcohol nuzzled his heart. He was moved, thinking of the small being who was on the way. Already he felt the tenderness of fatherhood. He looked at the children trailing around on the Square. His eyes misted over … . Fatherhood was beautiful!

At the post office Lepicq was writing:

'Soliciting legacy affair leaves me totally indifferent. You seem to forget that I'm on holiday! Regards'

He passed the form through the window. Reine Coulemelle leaned over the message, counted the words.

Several sessions lying in wait at a corner of the Patte-d'Oie-du-Petit-Roi had allowed Lepicq to notice that the same incomprehensible events repeated themselves each evening. After dinner, Reine Coulemelle went into her room, took off her everyday dress, tried various clothes and hats, settled her choice, made herself up with care, turned off the light and left the room.

But not the house!

Lepicq was sure of it. Did Reine Coulemelle go up to the married couple on the second floor where the husband was a joiner? Or to the tenants of the third floor, also a married couple; the husband was an employee of the Gas company, his wife the sister of Genêtou. That could have its importance?

After the absences of variable length, Reine Coulemelle went back into her room and settled down, as every day … .

'Four francs twenty-five, Sir,' the postmistress said.

Lepicq handed over a five franc piece, then changed his mind.

'I'd like to add some words.'

'Very simple!'

On the form Lepicq wrote:

'When is your engagement?'

'Four words more,' said Reine Coulemelle. 'That makes… .'

She had smiled. Because of the word engagement.

A secret smile, distant − like the look, the voice, the expression.

'Goodnight, Miss.'

'Au revoir, Sir.'

The clock stood at five past seven.

★ ★ ★

At Pibole's, Lepicq did not find Farjoux. They had telephoned from Rouen. It was not going very well at home. He had jumped on to his motor cycle and was gone. He begged Mr. Lepicq to excuse him.

Lepicq took his place again on the terrace, and ordered a second Pernod.

Close by some young men were seated at a table: butcher's assistants, baker's boys, day labourers … . They had already had plenty to drink. They were noisy. The dwarf was especially arousing their hilarity.

'D'you wanna bet that I do it?' A butcher boy with a flushed look suddenly said, in a thick voice.

'Bet you don't do it!'

He got up. He was tall as a wardrobe and big in proportion. He hitched up his trousers, leaned slightly to the right, then to the left, regained his balance and charged heavily at Couril. When he got to the same level he made a backhand grab, stealing the dwarf's hat. Then, with a deep laugh:

'Thousand apologies, baron!'

'Lout!' Couril retorted coolly.

'Whassat? Insults?'

'I repeat that you are a lout!'

Another got up.

'You'd like a good hiding? Ask the gentleman's pardon, right away!'

On the terrace Pibole was doubled up with laughter.

With great dignity the dwarf had picked up his hat and dusted it.

The butcher boy sent the hat spinning again.

'It's a thrashing you want?' He repeated. 'If it's that you want, I'll tan your hide! Dirty little pigs, that's my department!'

'You're stronger than me, the dwarf said in a calm voice. 'But I'm warning you in your own interest. If you touch me, I'll register a complaint.

'A complaint! Menaces now? Unpleasant! Nasty!'

With one hand the butcher boy seized the dwarf by the neck and pinned him to the trunk of a chestnut tree.

It was painful. On the terrace they were no longer laughing. They were waiting.

'Since the cops have not decided to bang you up, me, I'm going to send you to the hospital! You'll still be able to register your complaint, later!'

'I warn you … ', the dwarf spoke in a squeaky voice.

'Hey! Hey, down there! … . Just a minute! … '

This appeal of Prosper Lepicq stayed the butcher boy's hand, ready to make contact.

The lawyer went over with rapid steps. The boy let go of the dwarf, who remained stuck to the trunk of the tree.

'You, what do you want?'

'Leave this man in peace. Have you no shame?'

'No, but! What am I mixed up in! … .'

'You've been drinking! Go and lie down!' said Lepicq, repeating without thinking the same words that Zélie, taking him for Plainchant, had addressed to him in reponse to the number 64.

The lawyer made a lively jump to the side. The butcher boy's hand, large and red, passed some centimetres from his face. A second later, Lepicq's fist briefly met up with the cheek of the hulking lad who collapsed … .

He got up sheepishly, rubbing his somewhat injured jaw, all aggressive impulses snuffed out. On the terrace

Pibole was now laughing at him. It's always at the back of the loser that one laughs!

'I'm very obliged to you, my dear sir,' the dwarf spoke in his soft voice – his voice of long ago. 'But you shouldn't have to go to a lot of trouble … .'

★ ★ ★

After dinner, Lepicq offered Dorté and Genêtou a liqueur.

'Mr. Genêtou, do you know whether your sister is very friendly with Miss Coulemelle? They live in the same building, don't they?'

'Yes. But they never see each other. Coulemelle is not in contact!'

A few comments on the crime. Neither the secretary nor the clerk seemed very interested. Lepicq spoke obligingly of his work, mentioning really obscure affairs that he had nevertheless cleared up, terribly tricky cases, particularly thankless appeals which were nevertheless concluded to his credit, that's to say in the best interests of his clients. Shamelessly, he made his sales pitch. He even pointed out circumstances in which a guilty party had had the great fault of hesitating, of hanging about before making up his mind to seek his advice. Time lost is never made up. Don't put off until tomorrow what you can do today. Chance doesn't knock twice in succession at the same door. Opportunity has only one problem. All his chatter seemed to be only one persistent paraphrase – to his benefit – of the motto issued by the well-known fakir:

In trouble

Come to me.

Later he went to the Patte-d'Oie. Since his last trip to the post-office, an idea had come to him on the matter of the sessions of dressing and undressing.

The postwoman's room was not lit. It was too early.

'I think you are going the wrong way, my dear sir!'

Lepicq jumped. In the shadows that soft voice – Couril!

'Really, you think so!'

'Yes. Shall we walk a little? I'm going to tell you … .'

The thin lawyer and the pot-bellied dwarf strolled side by side.

'For a long time I interest myself in Reine Coulemelle … ,' Couril began.

'I've noticed it!'

'I study her. Shall I confess it to you, my dear sir? Like yourself, relatively speaking, I'm a curious spirit, on the lookout for the bizarre, for the unusual, the eccentric … .'

In consideration of Lepicq's long legs, Couril took long strides (long for a dwarf!). While Lepicq, from sympathy for the much reduced height of his companion, made excessively short steps, so much so that it was the dwarf who was in front, who had to slow the pace.

'What to do in a small town, unless one spies?' Couril joked. 'I spy. A small town, my dear master, what a marvellous hive of mysteries! Every window behind which a lamp shines suggests a puzzle! What of … .'

'Ah, that! … . It bothers me!' Lepicq reflected. There's a man of fine words!

They had barely moved out of Patte-d'Oie. Through rue du Pot-de-Grès, rue Gambetta, rue Gustave-Flaubert, the alleyway of the Square, rue Étourneaux, they described a circle of which the humble room of the postwoman occupied the centre.

'Reine Coulemelle – that manhunter, that hussy! Like they say! … . Do you know why she spends so much time in the evening, dressing up in front of her mirror? It's not for going to amorous meetings! Finally I understand!'

'Me too, I believe that I finally understand.'

'An old maid … .'

'But who has just passed forty! As a consequence a woman still young. And who sees only … .'

'You're there, my dear sir! Who sees alone. A shy one. A reserved type – reserved to the point of self-effacing.'

'A matter of hang-ups!'

'Hang-ups, that's it! Of repression, as they say in books! She's not ugly! She has blood which races, nerves that twitch …'

'And on her own!'

'And who always will be, my dear master! Ah well … . Ah well – no, in fact! She is not alone! In the end, she is she without being … .'

'Exactly what I was thinking,' Lepicq said. 'The wide-awake dream. The creation of ghosts. She is alone … with the ghosts!'

'Absolutely! The seductive ghosts who must, I imagine, be like film stars, like first young boyfriends … .'

They had come back onto Patte d'Oie. Reine Coulemelle's bedroom was lit. The postmistress was removing her working skirt, and slipping on an orange velvet dress.

'Forty years!' The dwarf spoke. 'That unused body! Those urges which come to the brain! The imagination which builds up a pretty dream and takes and fashions it, brings it into focus, caresses it indefinitely … . See there! She chooses her best dress, her prettiest hat, and makes herself up, makes herself beautiful … for dreaming of ghosts! She's created a world apart!'

'It's not foolish at all!' Lepicq said.

'A chimera … .' The dwarf spoke again.

'It's sad!' The lawyer murmured.

'I'm not that sure! She was used to it. She got into the habit of it. She placed herself in her dream! A dream which consists only of rosy colours! Nothing greyish, deceiving real life!'

The dwarf offered his podgy hand.

'My dear master, I wish you a good night. I will not manufacture sentences for telling you of my gratitude. Your intervention of this evening. When that drunk … . You pulled me out of a ridiculous position.'

'Let's leave that, shall we? Too happy to have been able … . Come, goodnight, Mr. Couril.'

The short silhouette melted into the shadows.

Only a moment later, Lepicq watched the little game of the postmistress.

In a little while she was going to put out the light and would pass into some bedroom decorated with photographs and, from there, she would be off in spirit … . That was her manner of gallivanting, of loose living!

Unless … . 'My sister? She and the Coulemelle woman never see each other!' Genêtou had affirmed.

And if, on the other hand, on the third floor, at the Gas employers home … .

The lawyer opened the carriage entrance of the rue des Étourneaux and took up position on the stairs at the precise moment when Reine Coulemelle blew out her lamp. He waited a long while.

The door of the postmistress's flat stayed shut. Cautiously, Lepicq went down, brushing the wall to avoid making the stairs creak.

As he was on the point of reaching the Hôtel Pibole:

'Sir … ,' whispered a voice issuing from the darkness. It was Couril – again!

'Can you give me five minutes? I have something which will interest you.'

'An hour! All night if you wish!'

'We're going to pass my place'.

The furniture was on the scale of the dwarf; seats at ground level, lilliputian table, doll's furniture, a Tom Thumb clock and a quantity of trinkets. The whole lot was furbished up, waxed, rubbed, polished, clean and gleaming.

Couril took from a drawer an envelope which carried no address. He opened it and let three strands of blue wool fall out which he handed over solemnly to Lepicq.

'What's that?'

'That will perhaps allow you to find Jaufre's murderer.'

The lawyer looked at it.

'I saw the murderer', the dwarf spoke in his soft voice.

'Good gracious! Who is it?'

'A woman. That's all I know. Around nine o'clock on the evening of the crime I went for a stroll. At the bottom of rue du Marché-Couvert I noticed the rear of Jaufre's house. I just found myself there. I saw the old man's kitchen door opening and a woman slipping into the yard, crossing it, and pushing the gate of the trellis fence which gives on to the outside. This woman had thrown a scarf over her head and was bent over. I wasn't able to make out her features, nor even get an idea of her age. She must have been still young because her movements were quick, so quick that she caught her skirt on the gate; she grabbed it and gave a tug. A minute later she had disappeared!'

'And you didn't follow her tracks?'

'Why would I have done that? I had no reason to consider that a crime had just ... .'

'That's right!'

'At the time, I attached no importance to what I had seen. I only noticed the details that I'm just giving you because I am, as I told you earlier, a curious soul. Provincial life, so short of events, ends up by making you a watcher! The fact of seeing a woman going out on the sly at such an hour from Jaufre's place which, strictly, is open only to Barnaby, seemed odd to me. Especially as there was no light in the old man's place! But the next day, when I had learned of the murder! ... . The murderer could only be the woman. She had waited for darkness before slipping away. I immediately went close to the gate in the trellis wall. It no longer holds up, it's been repaired with wire and was bristling with rusty nails. It's between two of these nails that I found these strands of wool.'

Lepicq eyed this tangible evidence of considerable value.

'Why have you not told the law?'

'I'm not a grass! Nor a "Friend of Truth"! For me, that

Jaufre is living or dead … . And for the interest that I take in the police!'

'But Barnaby! … . With a word, you could pull him out of prison!'

'He's as well off there as somewhere else.'

'Well, the indictment which is weighing on him … . Come, Mr. Couril!'

The dwarf made a vague gesture. Barnaby, Jaufre, the murderous woman, Criquebec and Criquebecians … . He lumped all these puppets together with the same contempt.

Lepicq sensed in this ill-favoured being, such a deep misanthropy, such a burden of disgust, such rancour, that he was painfully impressed.

'But yourself, Mr. Couril! The insinuations in which they have indulged themselves on your account! The anonymous letters?'

Another vague gesture, followed by a snigger.

'They can't prove that I am the originator of the murder, can they, since it's not true! So! The witch's sabbath? The wenching? That, that's a matter of private life! I don't take women by force! As a result … .'

He found his soft voice again.

'I made up my mind to tell you that, my dear sir, and to give you this evidence from sympathy. I'm not saying in gratitude for the service you have rendered me this evening. I'm saying sympathy.'

'I thank you very deeply.'

'Doubtless you are reckoning to tell the police? That would lead me to being muddled … . The judge would want me to account for my silence. People would harrass me a bit more. These threads of wool, couldn't you say you have found them yourself?'

'Understood! I reckon to occupy myself deeply in this affair. Also, I'll stay silent when I must. And when I speak it will not be with reference to you. I'll keep all the credit for myself … .'

103

CHAPTER 11

PROFESSOR ALFA

Professor Alfa opened an envelope bearing the Criquebec postmark. He pulled out two sheets of paper. Twenty lines in a woman's hand, tall and angular, covered the first page. The second, folded into eight contained, white on lamp black, the imprint of an index finger, a lock of hair tied into a favour, and a small square of chestnut-coloured fabric.

A smile lit up the face of the enigmatic Professor.

There was nothing mysterious about the office. No masks, no owls, tame or otherwise, no skulls, no magic figures. Filing cabinets, files. A young, blond girl was seated behind a glass table, the secretary.

Professor Alfa lit a cigarette, read the letter from Criquebec, his eyelids half closed. He then leafed through an elementary treatise on astrology.

'A special reply. You are ready, Miss Myra?'

'Yes, sir.'

'I dictate.'

(Incomplete horoscope dictated by Professor Alfa to Secretary Miss Myra.)

This Thursday, astronomical time 14.22'
Dear Madam,
It affords me real pleasure to give you here the precise study of your horoscope, which I have just finished. Your personality is stamped with great qualities; you are courageous, audacious and you do not lack ambition. Your mind allows you a lively

perception of artistic matters. Temperamentally highly mentally motivated … .

The Professor interrupted himself to stifle a yawn.

'Heck! What heat!'

He went to the window, leaned out over the boulevard Saint-Germain from which arose a hubbub – calls of car hooters, screeches of bus brakes.

The Professor resumed dictating:

All women are desirous of obtaining enlightenment on all the important questions which interest them, and with good reason. The detailed study of the hair and the fingerprint which you have sent me enables me to tell you that you are under the dominant influence of the South Pole. The Magnetic Irradiation of your Antarctic Circle and the magnetised Magnetic Snow in terms of your Sun, show that you will triumph over your enemy.

This twaddle was a response to the requests addressed to the Professor by Angèle Frelasset, the butcher's wife. These requests were as follows:

Professor Alfa, can you annihilate the business of a person who wishes me harm? The cards have already announced that a treacherous person is seeking to injure me, and I am entirely convinced as to who this person is. She is a pharmacist. Her first name is Aimée. I can tell you that she is a woman of wicked morals who is deceiving her husband! They say it's not just with one! I am telling you, I was able to record the little intrigue! If you could make a worthwhile accident happen to this woman, I would be very content.

I would also be truly content if you could win me a big prize in the National Lottery. I must confess to you that I have consulted other wizards before you but, until now, I have won nothing, despite doing all the draws, at times up to five tickets. Nothing happens! I have complete confidence in you. What numbers should

I pick and on what days should I buy the tickets?

Could you also increase my turnover? My firm is certainly the best meat purveyor in the town. But I would like to retire to go and live in Paris. One other thing; my husband often goes to the café to play cards, how can I cure him of this vice?

For the woman in question, the pharmacist, I am sending you a scrap of material that I took from an old dress which she used for rags. I think that that can be useful to you. Ask me for all the information of which you have need. Recently there has been a crime in this town. Could not this person have been there for something?

If you can reply favourably to me on these questions, I will know to recompense you; you will not have to complain of me.

In Criquebec Prosper Lepicq went to Mrs. Frelasset's home.

He had undertaken a series of visits. The tour of the Family Circle.

Nothing to get from his trip to the butcher's wife's house. She had bored him to tears on matters of the tarots, ink blots, etc … . In the morning, the pins had laid out an M and an H. H signifies 'drink nothing in your enemy's house'. M 'they wish for your end'… . The butcher's wife was certain that these warnings concerned someone other than herself. They were on the outside of a vast oval. 'Drink nothing. … . They wish for your end'. Who could be the threatened person?

On the other hand, what she was finding inside the oval greatly interested the butcher's wife. Two irregular squares, one large and one small. Significance: 'Someone is stopping your success!' She knew that anyway from long ago. The pins had not taught it to her. She even knew who: Aimé Gentil! But patience! They will laugh best who laugh last!

While chatting, she was playing with a large wallet of that impressive sort that horse dealers at trade fairs pull from their enormous pockets. The wallet was stuffed with notes –

and not small ones! Food is still doing as well as ever. People think first of their stomach!

She had offered coffee to the lawyer. A good filtered coffee.

By the way in which she stressed the F of filtered, one had the impression that she was saying 'A good Filtered coffee … .'

Professor Alfa was dictating to the secretary Miss Myra the rest of the partial Horoscope (astronomical time 14.40') of the butcher's wife.

What you request is perfectly possible. I can reduce your enemy to helplessness, setting her at odds with the people who listen to her lies, obliging her to leave the country, putting her business into a state of collapse … . I have a wonderful talisman of which I am not able to speak in my advertisements. If the antagonist resists it is a slow and serious illness for her, sometimes worse. It is worth 500 francs. This price only seems high. The rarity of the talisman, and its certain efficacy justifies it, and more. As far as Occult Works at a Fixed Rate *that you asked me about is concerned, it is difficult for me to specify to you the sum before having studied in depth the methods of achieving it. I see at your enemy's place a conjunction Mars-Moon which protects her strongly. But Venus is her weak point, we will reach her through that. As an indication, I am letting you know that the fee for the complete work such as you wish could never be less than ten thousand francs. It is not for a person like you with your intelligence that I need to underline the* FORMIDABLE DIFFICULTIES *of this business. But success is certain. I will be content however with a preliminary instalment of half the total: say five thousand francs.*

The letter concluded on a series of wily questions touching on the crime described by the butcher's wife.

★ ★ ★

Lepicq went to Vasseur's home. Seated on that stepladder with four steps that she climbed fifty times a day, the director of the *Wasp Waist* explained to him that the seven

Greek letters forming the magic word *Abraxas* give the number 365; the same number as there are days in the year! Then she said the sun was number ten and the symbol of infinity . The name of the emperor Nero Caesar written in ancient Hebrew gives 666, that's to say, the number of the Beast of the Apocalypse. Lepicq had leaned his right elbow informally on the shoulder of a charming young girl with a blossoming bosom. With the left hand he was carressing the waist of this agreeable person, who did not react. It must be said that she was wooden; she was the dummy upon which Vasseur tried out her corsets.

A woman of mature age came in. She wanted special support hose for her varicose veins. Lepicq slipped away.

For a while he paced up and down the Square, where the children were striving to set fire to various bits of paper, wisps of straw, and hairs on the hands, by means of a magnifying glass.

A blue dress … .

Lepicq had not seen one either at Vasseur's nor at Frelasset's. Nor, obviously, at the Maisondieus! For them the question did not arise; for twenty-four years they had not forsaken black! Lepicq had raised an eyebrow. 'And what if actually, so as not to be recognised, one or other of the sisters had put on a blue dress?'

He followed up his recapitulation.

Reine Coulemelle had two blue dresses. Mrs. Gentil one. Noémi none to his knowledge. Zélie often wore a blue dress. As for the widow Angat, she always wore blue, this being the colour of Jupiter.

But there were two hundred women in Criquebec. In what hanging cupboard, at the botttom of which wardrobe or in which trunk could be hidden the skirt from which the nails of the gate had torn three strands of wool?

Lepicq went into the *Wish to Please*. His plan was to tackle head on the question of the messages in numerals. But a complicated feeling held him back.

A boy and a girl appeared. They were clutching pennies in their fingers. The small girl wanted a stick of barley sugar.

'What colour do you want? Red? Blue? Yellow? Green?'

'The one with the most sugar please, Miss,' the girl babbled, intimidated by the presence of the lawyer.

Zélie had mostly green ones. She handed one over.

The boy asked for a firecracker. The cases were also coloured.

'What colour do you want?'

Colour mattered little to this young citizen.

'The one which goes off loudest!'

It was the yellow ones of which Zélie had the most; she handed over a yellow firecracker.

Then she raised her innocent eyes to the lawyer. 'Mrs. Beluge, I came to ask you … '.

She was smiling … .

No, asking the question about the coded messages was definitely not possible. Not at the moment … .

On the Square, the urchins were shouting eagerly; they had just succeeded in roasting the wings of a fly with their glass! Now they were going to do this with a spider.

'I will have need of a magnifying glass, Miss,' said Lepicq.

'Certainly, sir. I have three grades.'

'I'll take the strongest.'

★ ★ ★

THE HUMANITARIAN OFFER published in the *Yvetot Gazette* brought many requests for horoscopes to Professor Alfa. But only letters arriving from Criquebec held the wizard's attention.

'I am sixty years of age and on my own,' wrote one woman. *'I have modest means, having worked all my life and put*

some aside. *A young man has asked for my hand in marriage. He is twenty-five years old. Should I accept? Is he sincere, or is it from self-interest?'*

'Miss Myra,' Professor Alfa spoke, 'send the incomplete Horoscope number 4. Propose Talisman number 12. And will you add the following sentence:

'*I see that a crime has just been committed in your town. I have not learned of this through the papers; for more than ten years, for reasons of an impenetrable nature, I am formally forbidden to open a paper. This drama has been vouchsafed me through the Stars, while I was occupied in establishing the construction of your current Astral Sky. I have certain reasons for fearing the worries that could result for you from this murder, despite the fact that you have nothing to do with it. In your own interest, you will act wisely in letting me have all the observations that you have been able to make, information that you have been able to collect, even the tales which would seem to you insignificant. That will be useful to me in the astrological research which I propose to carry out on your behalf.'*

'You will underline '*in your interest,*' *if you please* Miss Myra.'

'*I am adding that the most absolute discretion is guaranteed you. I never keep a letter'.*

'Underline *never,* Miss Myra'.

Talisman number 12 was drawn 'ASTRAL FASCINATION ALFA' and accompanied by this commentary: '*Powder imported from Alaska. Gives a brilliant look, depth, attractive charm. Value 125 francs.'* Incomplete Horoscope number 4 ended as follows: '*The total amount of my fees for a very detailed complete Study is fixed at 150 francs. Although this price is quite minimal, as your case is one of the most interesting that I have had to study, I will give you the advantage of a preferential price of just fifty francs, on condition that your reply reaches me here in eight days at the latest.'*

The Professor opened another letter:

I would like to know about the evening job of a young girl whom I like and with whom I was angry because she formed an acquaintance last month at the charity fête, and now one often sees them together, which does not please me. She is called Jeanne. Can you tell me, from her handwriting, how far the thing has matured and whether this young girl has a relationship with this acquaintance?'

'Miss Myra, send incomplete Horoscope number 5 and propose Talisman number 9. Add the sentence on the subject of the murder in Criquebec.'

'Word for word?'

'Literally. Let's guard against being different!'

Horoscope number 5 ended just like Horoscope number 4: '*My fee is 150 francs. But your case is one of the more interesting ... . Only 50 francs ....*' Talisman number 9, a plaque upon which was engraved a magic love formula, was designated **ALFA MAGNETIC AZIMUTH**: Price 100 francs.

Another letter. Distressing.

'*Sick, with no money and just losing my job, I despair and am letting myself go. I have thoughts of suicide. I have need of moral help. I do not believe that after having worked so hard for fourteen years I am going to be repaid by the loss of my health. My husband is dead, in atrocious circumstances, and I have a child who is wasting for want of good food. I have a mortal dejection, I ache all over. Professor Alfa, I implore you, do not abandon me, come to my aid. If you knew how much I have confidence in you. Tell me what amount I must send you and I will pay it if I can.*'

Professor Alfa was not being a wicked man. He shook

his head sadly. But business is business and keeps us from pity as from individuality!

'Send incomplete Horoscope number 8, propose Talisman number 20.'

Horoscope number 8 is missing at present, sir. The printer was to deliver yesterday … .'

'Send number 9.'

Incomplete Horoscope number 9 – value 60 francs – was finally offered – cost to a friend – for the sum of twenty francs. And Talisman number 20: TAURUS ZODIACAL ALFA, was strongly suggesting purchasing '*luck, fortune, marvellous and unexpected situation, robust health,*' the whole lot for the trivial price of twenty-five francs.

'I put in the sentence concerning the crime?'

'Of course, Miss.'

★ ★ ★

'You'd never guess, Miss, what I'm about to ask!'

God! How sombre it was at the home of the elder of the Maisondieus.

The flat was stuffed with ancient furniture gathered by generations of Maisondieus. In the half light created by the heavy drapes drawn in a way to let the light enter only grudgingly, the portraits on the walls made one think of stern ghosts. They were defunct Maisondieus, all those who had contributed to the establishment, to the enrichment and embellishment of the vast house. This one had brought two tables, a wardrobe, a bed, a clock. That one a sideboard, a rich collection of kitchen equipment, sheets, tablecloths, a clock. Another vases, carpets, books on law (that was Hippolyte Maisondieu the solicitor) a small clock and its glass globe, a clock. Another, pious images, very old flowered plates which were worth a good sum, artistically forged iron fire dogs, a clock.

Each one had brought his clock, the same rustic model,

heavy, enclosed inside a tall wooden case. It was only the wood that was different – sometimes walnut, sometimes cherrywood, sometimes oak. Each marriage had corresponded with the arrival of a clock. They were there in all the rooms, often two in the same room. Like this from the top to the bottom of the building. All the clocks worked. Every Saturday, Amandine carefully wound them. The house, filled with ticking, seemed itself to be just a gigantic machine for measuring out time.

Amandine Maisondieu put down her knitting work.

'And what have you come to ask me, Sir? A consultation! Would it bore you to give me a reading of the lines of the hand?'

A strong odour of mothballs drifted. The wardrobes were filled with relics – old coats, antique feathered hats; they had to preserve all that from clothes moths and the larvae. None of this which had belonged to a Maisondieu, of this which had been bequeathed by a Maisondieu, of this which recalled a Maisondieu, must be abandoned to decay. Amandine was the vigilant guardian of Maisondieu relics. Every month she made an inspection, stuffing mothballs into the drawers under piles of linen … .

She had grasped the lawyer's left hand with restrained eagerness; put it down carefully like an infinitely fragile object onto a pedestal table, and had leant over it, she had, so to speak, smelled it. No good increasing the gap of the curtains. In the provinces, by virtue of delaying to the last moment the lighting of the lamps, everyone developed a little day blindness!

She spoke in her masculine voice:

'In your childhood, your days were put in danger by a serious illness.'

'That's right. Typhoid. I was thirteen.'

A line of shadow was giving to Amandine's inclined face a jawline beard!

Lepicq reflected that since the typhoid, his days had

very often been put in danger. Not through illness! Through pistol shots and knife attacks … .

On the square, it was very warm. Here, it was fresh, almost cold.

Amandine's bony fingers rested on Lepicq's palm, pressed the Mount of Mars, the Mount of Venus, the Mount of the Moon, lingered in the Great Quadrangle, and stopped in the Supreme Angle formed by Head and Life lines.

She raised her sallow face.

'Towards your fiftieth year I foresee an accident concerning your lower limbs.'

'Illness?'

'I believe not.'

'Accident?'

'Injury rather. I see a clean cut. Be in fear of daggers, axes and scythes. All sharp instruments.'

She looked at him intently. It must have been with such a look and in this doleful voice that Amandine Maisondieu, one day in the twilight, had confided to the widow Angat 'A cardiac accident will carry your husband off early.'

As always, she was in black. All the Maisondieus that one saw in the portraits were in black. The wallpaper was dark, the draperies and the chair coverings were all sombre.

Lepicq pondered that perhaps at the bottom of one of these wardrobes, there was a woollen dress, a blue dress … .

'The days must seem to you long at times, Miss?' He spoke when the consultation had finished.

'Why?' She asked simply.

'You live so withdrawn … .'

'I'm very well on my own. I am not one of those who has need of the company of others.'

'Your sister settled herself a long time ago Miss, in her house near the church?'

'Since the death of our parents, that's twenty-four years. Each in their own place, isn't that so? It's so much better!'

Twenty-four years, alone, to have to have in your ear

these countless tick-tocks of the clocks…

Lepicq felt cold. He wasn't long in leaving and went up to Clémence's home.

Her feet on a foot warmer, she was shivering.

'I believe I have the fever. I had a nasty nightmare. I was in Yvetot. All of a sudden, I'm falling on Andréa Gauric, the school mistress. Or rather, I'm falling on the head of Andréa: this head was advancing along the pavements by small jumps. "And where are you taking yourself like that, my dear girl?" I say. "Have you noticed that you left your body on the way? You're mad! – I'm going to my milliner," Andréa tells me. "I've left my body at the house. Why would I have dragged it to as far as here, I have no need of it since I'm going try on a hat! I've had enough of my head! – but unfortunately you walk between people's legs!" I say, "Someone is going to step on a cheek!". "You must be joking," she says. "People look where they're putting their feet! And for a start, everybody knows me here!" I would very much like to know,' Clémence concluded, 'what this dream meant! I found nothing in the Golden Key of the Egyptians.'

The house was very much smaller than that on the Square, and furnished barely. One got a feeling of a provisional arrangement. As though Clémence was simply camping out here, awaiting the death of Amandine, the moment when she would be able to go down onto the Square, into the true Maisondieu house, to take possession there and install herself in it. Twenty-four years this temporary arrangement was lasting, while she waited, skirt fallen around her footwarmer which did not prevent her from shivering, despite the scorching heat. Twenty-four years in which she kept her gaze fixed on the crossroads from where one saw a stone bench, the three steps of the church, Lecorbin's pump which no-one used , and the road leading down to the Square … .

In Clémence's house there was no collection of clocks.

Just one small one on the fireplace in a gloomy corner. On the other hand, Lepicq noticed lying under the cushions, on the seats, a large number of cats of both sex, all stuffed. The taxidermist had set them in an attitude of sleep. All the cats that Clémence had raised and cherished during her lifetime!

The ticking of the small clock was so discreet that one did not hear it.

'I dare not look at the clock any more! I'm afraid to think that night is coming, that I'm going to have to go to bed, fall asleep, and dream. I always wonder what nightmares I'm going to have. It's specially terrible in the winter; the days are so short!'

Down below, the smell of mothballs. Here, the odour of the chemist's shop. On the table, within hand's reach, Clémence always kept medicaments – drops, small pills, larger pills, potions … .

Her face was more tired, more crumpled than usual.

Lepicq still reflected on the blue woollen dress.

'The idea of living with Miss Maisondieu your sister would not please you?'

'It wouldn't be possible. We like each other well enough, but on condition of only seeing each other like this, in passing!'

'Hullo!' Lepicq said to himself,' they're not all stuffed!'

One of the tomcats had just raised it's head, yawned and stretched. It was thin with a poor coat.

'I have eight stuffed and three living' Clémence said. 'When I say living … they behave like me; they crawl about!'

Her face took on an expression at the same time mysterious and frightened.

'At the widow's house they mock me for my fears. But me, I know!'

From a murmur she went on to a whisper:

'I'm certain that someone is seeking to poison me by

inches. I have the impression that even the air I breathe contains poison. My cats are sick just like me! One day they will find the proof … .'

'Perhaps you are not well enough ventilated?'

'I keep my windows closed in the daytime, to have less noise, but I sleep every night with the window wide open behind my shutters!'

She took a small pill.

'We'll see you shortly at the widow's ?'

'Certainly,' the lawyer said.

'So … Later.'

Lepicq passed on to the *Good Swordsman*.

Plainchant showed him a model of the knife which had been used to murder Jaufre.

'I sell more than a hundred in a year! To the people of Criquebec, to the peasants of the villages. And I have dealers who look out for me at fairs, markets … .'

He showed the lawyer a dozen or so knives so small that they could together be accommodated readily in a cherry stone.

'I make them myself. I do this to amuse myself.'

These knives were amazing ! No larger than a grain of millet. And each one had its blade fixed by a pin to the grooved handle! They opened and shut! They were so incredibly light that he needed to take care not to breathe too heavily, they could have blown away! Lepicq examined them with magnifying glass number 3 that he had bought at the *Wish to Please*.

All these visits were beginning to wear him out. He abandoned for the moment going to Dr. Pouacre's home. He had had occasion, on several visits, to chat with the pallid doctor. Pouacre did not stop talking of illness, but it was of his own that he spoke! One had the feeling that the rôles were reversed, that the doctor was asking you for a consultation and that on parting he would put his hand in his purse and would ask you 'How much do I owe you, doctor?' This Pouacre, so pale, so limp, with his three blond hairs on his chest … .

Lepicq went to greet the widow Angat.

She was drinkng borage tea – an eminently favourable herb for Jupiterians.

'I can't offer you a cup, sir? I expect you'll prefer your apéritif! You're quite right!'

'I must confess to you that … .'

They laughed. The widow was a relaxing person in whose company one felt inclined to look on the bright side of life.

'The construction of your birth sky will soon be finished, my dear sir. I have already noted interesting things.'

'And on the whole?'

'It's rather good. In House I you have a Sun-Mars conjunction, reinforced by Mercury in joy, which … .'

'What a bother you are giving yourself!'

'Not at all! It's a pleasure! Ah! … One question! Have you not had the misfortune of losing your parents very early on?'

'Alas, yes!'

'I'd have sworn it! Saturn and the Moon at ninety degrees in House VIII … .'

* * *

Lepicq had installed himself in front of a brandy on the terrace of the Pibole.

From the tour of the town which he had just taken he had not learned anything. He was not disappointed. He could not have expected to learn anything definite. He had avoided any question, indeed any allusion to the murder. Only Plainchant had touched on the subject, by reference to the knife. Lepicq had not given him the answer. He did not care to speak of the crime! Seeing the people … , above all, seeing their homes and watching in the light or the shade of their interiors to discover that slight difference

118

there always is between such gestures, such attitudes, such intonations and these same gestures, these same attitudes, these same intonations, depending upon whether one is at home, in the homes of others, or in the street ... . Knowing individuals from the setting they gave themselves, finding out their character from the colour of the wallpaper, their furniture, their taste in carpets, or their passion for waxed parquet flooring.

The look, the innocent smile of Zélie, dealer in firecrackers, her lollies! The butcher's ruddy wife and her pocket book crammed with notes! Vasseur, whose shop was so trite that it left in Lepicq's mind only one image; the wooden girl, the dummy for trying on corsets! The icy austerity of the Maisondieu's house. The installation so paradoxically provisional of Clémence's establishment, and this collection of cats of which one could not distinguish those living from those who were dead, those who slept with only one eye, for five minutes, from those who slept on both ears, for ever! Médéric Plainchant ... . His tiny, feathery knives, which were laid down by the dozen in a cherry stone, and which blew away with a breath ... .

For the greatest pleasure of his palate and the greater harm of his liver, but with the consent of his conscience, Lepicq sampled his three-star brandy. A voice told him he had not wasted his time.

He even had an acute moment, one of those fleeting instants of sublime lucidity, touching on the divine, in which he felt with an unusual potency that he had gone from less than nothing to a breath of the truth. Someone, with a phrase having no connection with the crime, had offered him the key, had led him to the edge of the solution ... .

But what phrase?

'In fact,' he said to himself. 'I still have a visit to make!'

Through the rue du Marché-Couvert, he reached the yard of Jaufre's shanty. The kitchen door was not locked – he knew that. He went into the house.

It was to the dead that he was making this visit. To the ghost of Jaufre.

Without disturbing what was there, he went through the rooms: dining room, office, book collection, bedroom. A thick layer of dust covered the mouldy furniture, the dog-eared books. In the bedroom, a trapped wasp was buzzing and careering about. Because of its rapid flight and the too bright light, it was hardly visible and one thought of a small irritated spirit … .

★ ★ ★

Professor Alfa continued to go through the copious mail which arrived from Criquebec.

A letter from Fernande Vasseur. The devotee of numbers insisted that the wizard studied her special case from the viewpoint of values – favourable or ill-fated. Furthermore she requested the means of rendering a brutal husband gentle. The Professor despatched to her, via the secretary Miss Myra, incomplete Horoscope number 6, offering Talisman number 17: SPHINX OF THE ICES, and put the question relating to the crime.

A letter from Zélie Beluge. She wished above all that the wizard tell her her most favourable flower.

'Incomplete Horoscope number 11, Talisman 11: GREAT ARCTIC CIRCLE, and the question relating to the crime'.

A letter from Médéric Plainchant. Had he or had he not to give up his shop? Someone had made him an offer. He was hesitating. Furthermore, he was considering getting married. But, at his age, was this not a foolish thing?

'Incomplete Horoscope number 8.'

' Eight is missing, sir.'

'Give number 7, Talisman: LAPLANDER RING. And the question relating to the crime'.

A letter from Amandine Maisondieu. She requested the date of her death and that of her sister.

120

'Horoscope number 4. Talisman: MIDNIGHT SUN. And the question … .'

A letter from Clémence. She requested the explanation of two nightmares, a talisman against harmful dreams, another against poisons, and the date of her death, as well as the date of the death of her sister.

'Horoscope number 5. Talisman: MAGIC SNOW. And the question … .'

A letter from Dr. Pouacre. He was worried. About his health. Requested psychical treatment.

'Horoscope number 7. Talisman: SOUTHERN EXPLOSIVE ALFA. And the question … .'

A letter from Francis Couril. The dwarf requested a method for developing will and boldness.

'Does there really exist a way of becoming master of the fluid forces which are within us, and could I succeed in using it in such a way to offset my physical inferiority and to put down my enemies? Equally, I would be very obliged to you for being willing to speak to me on the question of love. How to fight against shyness? How to approach women with the best chances of pleasing them?'

'Horoscope number 6. Talisman: SOUTHERN CROSS. And the question …'

A letter from Mrs. Angat. A letter from Mrs. Pibole. A letter from … Noémi – the sceptic!

'Horoscope number so and so. Talisman number so and so. Horoscope number so and so. Talisman number so and so. And the question. And the question. And the question. … . Make haste Miss Myra! Time is money!'

★ ★ ★

After tea at the widow's there was a séance around the circular table. Several spirits presented themselves that no-one had called at all, and who seemed really poorly attached to their identity. They spoke of being Napoleon and, a moment later, denied it. 'So, who are you? Louis II of

Bavaria? Louis II of Bavaria, yes, that's it! You're really sure? Not that certain! You wouldn't sometimes be Margaret of Burgundy! Yes, yes! I'm Margaret of Burgundy!'

It wasn't serious. These defunct beings made preposterous declarations. They were simply spirits, not to say simple spirits. There were also the jokers, the fantasists from the beyond, the phoneys that even the great leap had not been able to subdue.

But, finally, they had Jaufre.

He was weary, weak, disoriented, still not adapted to the other world. His passage from earthly existence to astral life had been hard going. He was seriously put off by the shock. They put to him the question relating to the crime.

'Is Barnaby really your murderer?'

'No.'

'Do you want to name your murderer?'

'No.'

So the assassin will remain unpunished?'

'No.'

'Do you wish to say that they will discover the murderer?'

'Yes.'

That was all for that day.

These women then spoke of Professor Alfa. What did Lepicq think of this wizard in the polar hat?

'I admire experts,' the lawyer said. 'I respect people who give themselves over to serious studies (here, a bow towards the widow who blossomed, flattered). But I reckon that they would not know enough to mistrust individuals who, too often, only give themselves the air of talking about the stars, the better to blackmail people!'

CHAPTER 12

FRIENDS OF THE TRUTH

'As to the crime, I would hardly be able to tell you much, Professor. Like the Stars you attested to I am not involved, nor anyone close to me. The man who has been murdered was a good fellow, who did good things for his town. A mute has been arrested but they start to prattle at the expense of a dwarf. He is a hateful being, very spiteful. They are saying that … . There are those that have written to the judge to say that … . Nowadays, you know, tongues … .'

Every day Professor Alfa received replies like this. This person clearly interested himself greatly in the puzzle of Jaufre's death, as did Lepicq and Farjoux. He was an intelligent man and knew that people innocently confide in the first seer come across, little as he knew you, to inspire trust in secrets that one would not reveal to a doctor, not even to a priest. Setting the inhabitants of the small locality, one against the other and, through the network of the scandalmongering and the slander, to discover the answer to the mystery, that appeared to be his purpose. But then?

'Getting the stars to speak so as to blackmail people better!' Attractive formula!

'Miss Myra, let me have the list of people who have not replied to our despatch of an incomplete Horoscope with a request for a complete Horoscope.'

'Here, sir.'

Amongst others not replying ; Zélie Beluge, Mrs. Angat, Lecorbin, Plainchant, Gratoulet, Genêtoul, Couril.

'Couril … . The dwarf about whom they prattle! He

123

wanted a method for overcoming shyness I believe?'

'Yes, sir. And recipes for approaching and seducing women!' Miss Myra replied smiling.

She was a lovely creature. Under the table she stretched her extremely beautiful legs, sheathed in very fine silk. The dress, rather short, disclosed a hint of knee. Professor Alfa rested a dreamy look on these disturbing legs. But in truth he did not see them. He was seeing a small town in lower Normandy, cruelly scoured by the sun, prostrated with torpor, and which he had undertaken to knock for six.

'You will send our formula Number 2 to everyone who has not followed up on their first letter.'

'You have neglected to respond to the outline of your life (formula number 2 noted). I am very disappointed in noticing your indifference concerning your happiness, and am not hesitating to rebuke you. If I am writing to you afresh, it's because I know that you are going to have to confront certain very imminent events which will have an exceptional importance for you. The Stars tell me that you will have to pass through a painful passage, for which my advice would be invaluable for you.

Don't forget that your complete Horoscope is a document that you will have to purchase only once in your life. For proving to you all the affection that your personnage inspires in me, and so as to allow you to acquire more readily the Work that I wish to carry out on your behalf, I ask you to send me only the modest payment of thirty francs. Do not let this opportunity pass.'

★ ★ ★

Almost a week had passed since the day Lepicq had undertaken a round of visits. Since then, he had received a despatch from Jugonde:

'Sending you documentation on Bezons inheritance appeal. Very interesting business. When are you returning?'

In fact shortly after, the documentation had arrived in a large envelope. Lepicq had shrugged his shoulders.

★ ★ ★

At the widow Angat's home, the séances continued to be held regularly. Vasseur complained that her husband was becoming more and more irascible.

'Make him take some tossed green balm with cypress sap in his soup', advised Zélie. 'That makes the worst brutes milder!'

They did table-turning. Jaufre came or didn't come. They could get hardly any information. One day, Clémence gave warning that they had not to count on her; she was unwell. That got a long laugh from the women! They were used to Clémence's illnesses! Angèles Frelasset moaned because her storeroom was infested with rats.

'Burn some horse hoof! There's nothing they fear more!' Zélie recommended.

★ ★ ★

Lepicq went up to see Clémence. She had taken to her bed. The three surviving tomcats were sleeping on her eiderdown and were scarcely any better than their mistress. The lawyer was shaken to see the old girl a cyanosed colour, almost blue. She was breathing with difficulty, feeling suffocated, and dizzy.

'This burns me in the chest, Mr. Lepicq. They are trying to poison me. Someone has sworn to poison me. They look down on me, but … .'

'Well me, I believe you!' Lepicq burst out briskly. 'Someone is poisoning you by degrees. I'm convinced of it!'

Terrified, she sat up.

'Who? You have found him out?'

'I think so, Miss.'

'Who is it?'

'These!' The lawyer indicated the eight stuffed cats. 'I presume you have always gone to see the same taxidermist?'

'Yes. A man from Havre. He does good work.'

'Right! But I fear that he has the unfortunate habit of treating the skins that one entrusts to him with arsenious acid! Either I very much deceive myself or you have chronic poisoning!'

'That's not possible! These pussycats … .'

'These pussycats saturated with arsenic however, are poisoning the air of this room! That must be the origin of your recurrent nightmares. Ventilating the room at night, you wake up less tired. But during the day you shut your windows – poisoning starts again! Will you entrust one of these animals to me?'

The analysis which Mrs. Gentil undertook confirmed Lepicq's suspicion. Clémence got up, hollowed out a pit in her garden, and buried the tomcats there.

★ ★ ★

Two days passed.

The morning of the third day, when the lawyer went into the dining room of the hotel, to take his breakfast, he saw Mrs. Pibole with a delighted expression.

'You ought to hurry over to the Square, Mr. Lepicq!'

Surprised, he went over. Everyone was on their doorsteps. Groups were gathered.

'What are they waiting for?'

'The dwarf, to see the face he makes when he sees the writing!'

'Writing?'

'Someone fixed it on a chestnut tree last night. It must be the butcher's assistant that you thrashed … .'

The lawyer had quickly spotted the item of general interest; a large sheet of cardboard fixed at about two metres high. In the middle, in large capitals, this accusation:

COURIL THE MURDERER!

The dwarf appeared. He soon saw the placard. They were laughing below it. He went slightly pale, ground his teeth, turned, and went back to his home.

'He's going to look for a stick to pull the notice down!'

It was his hat that the dwarf was going to fetch. He went off quickly. Twenty minutes later he was back; he brought the village policeman.

'Mr. Aubin, I want you to take notice … .'

He went back indoors and came out again with a chair onto which he clambered. But even perched like that he was still too short! Aubin had to take down the cardboard placard himself. The two men then went up to the Town Hall.

Lepicq went with them; it was an excellent opportunity to see Genêtou again.

Couril wrote in due form a complaint of defamation against an unknown. He had to make a rough draft, breaking off frequently to enquire of Lepicq his opinion on the precise meaning of such and such a judicial term; he was very suspicious of the form.

He then threw his rough draft into the basket.

Lepicq was studying the defamatory inscription with the magnifying glass.

Suddenly, the glass set aside, he made a grimace.

'That would be too much! … .'

The dwarf and Aubin had withdrawn. Genêtou was hunting through old birth certificates, with a view to statistics (Lecorbin's hobby). He turned his back on Lepicq. The latter went quietly to take from the basket the rough draft of Couril's written complaint and slipped it into his pocket.

'Mr. Genêtou, do you see any inconvenience in my

examining this exhibit for a moment?' He spoke later, showing the writing in capitals.

'Certainly not, Mr. Lepicq!'

'I'm going to install myself at the café opposite. I'll report to you in a quarter of an hour … .'

'When it suits you, Mr. Lepicq!'

From professional necessity the lawyer had made serious studies of handwriting. Comparison of the capitals of the writing with those found in Couril's draft revealed surprising similarities.

'It could be uncanny all the same!'

Couril the author of the writing which accused him! Couril perching on a stool at night to stick the notice to the trunk of a chestnut tree and next morning lodging a complaint! To what purpose this bewildering act?

But actually … . The anonymous letters revealing the dwarf's depravity, depicting him as a person of dissolute morals? Possibly Couril himself, was he the author of one of them?

Lepicq telephoned the police station at Yvetot.

'Was Inspector Farjoux supposed to be returning soon from Rouen?'

'He came yesterday evening. Actually he's here. I'm passing him to you; hold on.'

'Hallo? Mr. Lepicq.' Farjoux trumpeted. 'I'm very pleased to hear you! It happened, have you heard? It's a boy! He arrived the day before yesterday; it happened without any trouble! At last … almost! We're calling him Camille, as agreed. The funniest thing is that the mother obstinately maintains that she always wanted a boy, whilst in reality … . Women don't know either what they say nor what they want! But I'm babbling … . When do I see you?'

'In half an hour!'

'Eh?'

'In half an hour! I'm leaving by car in a moment.'

'There's something new?'

'No! Simply I've had enough of Criquebec!'

'Good idea! I'm waiting for you. We're going to have a first class lunch. I've discovered a club which doesn't look much but where there's a little Arbois … .'

★ ★ ★

By three o' clock in the afternoon, Lepicq had seen the anonymous letters and drawn his own conclusion, without having mentioned a word of his suspicions to Farjoux.

Without any possible doubt Couril was one of the most active amongst the *Friends of the Truth*! He was the author of at least four of those missives which dragged him through the mud!

Lepicq made his return to Criquebec in time for the widow's tea. Zélie Beluge was furious.

'That Professor Alfa is the absolute limit! I had asked him to tell me my favourite flower, so as allow me to take account of his worth as a seer because there isn't much he could teach me on the matter of flowers! So Alfa indicates the dahlia to me. Now, do you know what dahlia signifies, from the language of the Flowers? *Many words, little soul!* That's the flower that he recommends to me! This lad's an idiot!'

Lepicq was musing on Couril.

What game was the dwarf playing?

Suppose that he's the murderer. He admits to going wenching, of organising the nocturnal witch's sabbaths. None of all that is true; the police will have readily understood that. Couril later admits to being the murderer. They'll be bound to consider the writing in relation to the anonymous letters. And they'll not seriously suspect the dwarf. But if he has killed, why not very simply stay quiet? And why has he told me this story of the woman in the blue dress? To lull me into a feeling of false security?

'You seem very cheerful, Mr. Lepicq?'

The lawyer jumped. It was true. He had assumed a blissful air to stare at the ceiling! ... .

'Excuse me! I was dreaming of this seer who had recommended the dahlia to Mrs. Beluge! He must be stupid!'

Alfa had just rendered the lawyer a great service! The latter had finally understood the significance of the coded messages that Zélie and Plainchant addressed to one another!

The Language of Flowers ... .

In the bookshop Lepicq bought a booklet of some dozen pages. On the decorated cover a bouquet in frenetic colours. In it he found a numbered list of almost 500 flowers.

Of course! It could only be that, their 'Code'! They were sending off numbers corresponding to the chosen flowers. An original way of saying 'Good day! Good night!'

A platonic idyll between the two sexagenarians ... . And this mischievousness of Zélie, who knew her flowers, who dreamed of flowers, had one day had this comical creation; to correspond in the language of flowers! Plainchant, stupid old man, had very much wanted to fall in with the fun!

'Let's see now! The evening when I slipped into the cutler's place and where I so affronted Zélie, I had first of all written 46. She had laughed, then replied 182. Next, I sent 64. And she told me to go and lie down!'

His finger ran along the list.

46 (Common Teasel) *I thirst for you!* Hang it all! It was flirting actually! I understand that she had laughed!

His finger again slid over the pages.

182 (Saffron) *I remember you with restraint!*

It's good that! That hits it off admirably! But what can 64 mean?

Some seconds later he burst out laughing. It explained Zélie's indignation.

64 (Yellow wallflower) *I would like to clasp you in my arms!*

Crikey! That was more than amorous! It was … rakish!

Éros … .A malicious little Éros, such was the master of reticence!

126 (Water Lily) *You are ice!* Telegraphed, to tease the man of the *Fine Swordsman*.

166 (Rhubarb) *Do not lose courage!* The woman from the *Wish to Please* replied ironically.

Then a regret came over her.

101 (Mauve lilac) *Do you still love me?*

He flared up. She resumed her teasing:

107 (Lupin) *Leave me alone. I have need of peace!*

He was stung:

50 (Eucalyptus) *You have an unpleasant character!*

In this way the butterflies had led Lepicq to Criquebec.

Then he had been kept in this town by mysteries which were not there. The lively banter of two sexagenarians, a postwoman who, every evening, made herself attractive for no-one!

And a real mystery had set itself up; a bloody mystery of which he still did not have the key, a kitchen knife savagely planted in the neck of an old man … .

★ ★ ★

Professor Alfa intensified his activity.

All the scandals which make the rounds of a small town, the origin rarely clear cut! The fortunes, the ambition of this one, the meanness of that one, the nasty illness of this official, the loose behaviour of the wife of this municipal councillor, and that one stealing, that one so much on the edge of bankruptcy, all the roguery which flowered under the Criquebec sun, all the treachery that a smiling face hides, the smell of the corrupted which lifts the spirits, the Professor had put all that on file which Miss Myra the secretary with the nice legs sorted. At present he knew Criquebec like the end of his finger, like Zélie knew the flowers! He was able to go strolling there, eyes shut, knocking on doors:

'Mr. F … . Isn't it? It's actually you who sold those cows, feet burning with tuberculosis, and those pigs dying of erysipelothrix? Congratulations! Ah, it isn't you Mr. L … who stole 100,000 francs from the Government last year on a certain matter of careers? Nice work! Hallo! This good Mr. G … cuckolded, beaten and content! Delighted to shake your hand Mr. G. … .'

To those who, like Couril, Lecorbin and the widow Angat, insisted in not replying to their first letter, the Professor set about sending his most imperative phrases:

'You are acting against your interests. *I see in your Sky a conjunction of Planets which announce sombre days for you before long. I will agree to reduce my offer to the derisory price of twenty francs, which does not even cover the costs of writing and of the secretariat. I cannot save you against your will! So write to me before I regret such an offer, without which, it will no longer be possible for me to involve myself with you, and your future must suffer.'*

★ ★ ★

Menace was breaking out.

In Criquebec, this campaign was bearing fruit. The spite, the malice was increasing. By virtue of the Professor's letters, the climate was taking on these immeasurable qualities which preside over sly shifts of emphasis and insensibly transform an air of comedy into one of drama. The spiteful Genie of Allusions was organising a game which was played by choice in private, behind the cover of blinds, of awnings. With the coming of dusk, it gained in virulence. In the bleary light of candle-ends, at the edge of the malevolent shadow of vast chests pressing without creasing the clothes and with lovers, it grew richer with elements of savagery, under the eye and with the assent of the family portraits hung on the walls like so many sarcastic rogues. Even good feelings turned to vinegar in hearts. In the inkwells the ink was turning to vitriol!

★ ★ ★

At the widow Angat's home, the séances in the Uranus room became passionate and frenetic; the female knights of the round table made the pedestal table waltz with a vengeance, heave-ho! And clamouring for Jaufre with might and main!

In town, they were waxing indignant.

Because Jaufre's popularity was growing.

They no longer spoke of giving his name to a street, but that scarcely delayed them. They had constructed an elegant inscription to him in the cemetery, and his tombstone was decked sumptuously with flowers. At present there were ten indigent old folk in the Rest Home. All fat as bacon, well turned out and overjoyed, nourished like friars, happy as Popes. On Sundays people went up to visit them. The visitors were conducted there. They were the heart-warming livestock of Criquebec.

One morning the widow Angat found the following notice traced in tar on her door, shutters and walls:

> *Committee of the Friends of Jaufre*
> To the widow Angat and other old trout:
> A Sound Piece of Advice
> If you do not want to have worries
> Leave the table turning in peace!
> THE DEAD WOULD LIKE TO SLEEP!

No signature of course! The work of a *Friend of the Truth* again.

Noémi was going to have a full day's work getting rid

of this writing with a scraper, brush and petrol.

'It's a disgrace! An absolute scandal!' The widow raged in the Jupiter room in front of the dismayed servant and Lepicq, shaken with internal laughter.

'The other day Couril ... Now, me! But they won't ever catch him, the wretch who ... . Pity Jaufre is no longer alive! He would have found the villain out!'

How's that? Lepicq wondered.

'I'm going to tell you something that very few know, my dear sir. Jaufre kept himself busy with graphology.'

'Ah pooh!'

'He admitted it to me one day. I understood his intention very well; he was hoping that I would invite him to take part in our circle. We deal with all the sciences revolving round the character of man. Ah well, graphology ... . Jaufre had said "Finding these women in Mrs. Angat's sitting room, chattering, discussing ... ." That would have flattered him! Mind you, if it had been someone suitable, I would have been the first to ... . But, just between ourselves, old Jaufre was unsavoury! That's not because they are making him a saint at this moment! Briefly! When I saw his advances, I did something which wasn't understood!'

She was going to start fulminating again about the unknown with the tar, but Lepicq's manner cut short her complaints at their source. The lawyer leapt for his hat, spluttered words of excuse, reached the door, and dashed off.

'What's taken him?' Noémi wondered. 'He left the gas on?'

Lepicq's manner had the air of victory. He tore through the steep roads like a runner spotting the winning post. He was nearing his goal. He was about to know! Aha, old Jaufre took an interest in the study of handwriting! ... . Ah well, the *Friends of the Truth* would have served the truth after all, without suspecting it!

He went into the solicitor's office. Doré was writing up

134

an attestation for the transfer of a lease. A young assistant was stamping envelopes.

Lepicq's manner was such that Doré suddenly felt himself ill at ease. Scenting trouble, he directed a troubled look towards a curtain of faded red velvet. Lepicq indicated the assistant and made a meaningful gesture with his hand.

'Sonny,' Doré spoke hastily, 'slip down to the stationers and get some gum arabic. And buy me a book of stamps and a packet of cigarettes.'

Lepicq sat himself without ceremony on a corner of the desk. He pointed to the curtain. 'Is that Mr. Figuier's office behind that?'

'Yes.'

'Mr. Figuier is there?'

'Yes.'

Lepicq sniggered.

'Do you care hugely about losing your position, Mr. Doré?'

'Um!' … . The other man jumped. 'You're joking. I … .'

'You conned me, Doré! The day the crime was discovered – the trick with the brief case at the café; very cunning!'

'Don't speak so loud!' Doré whispered, 'Mr. Figuier could … .'

He had become crimson.

'You had realised that I suspected you of having made a document vanish. You had made the first move, obligingly opening up your briefcase! It was crammed with some of the documents! But … only the documents of the study! Of the "classification work!" Very clever! And Genêtou did the same!'

Doré tried to evade the issue.

'I promise you, sir … . I don't see where you want … .'

He squinted in desperation at the edge of the red curtain.

'That's enough! Listen. Jaufre was involved in graphology.

The alphabet was his passion! Just a moment before his death, he was amusing himself with experiments on letters, disguising them as numerals, on the back of a postcard! But that was a diversion. To feed his harmless hobby, Jaufre had need of handwritten texts. Of texts without value in themselves; interesting only in that they were revealing the character of their authors. D'you follow me, Doré? No good shaking your head! ... . How to get hold of documents, of old letters? Whom to ask? Everyone disliked Jaufre!'

'Having noticed that a certain Doré, solicitor's clerk, and a certain Genêtou, the mayor's secretary, were considerable boozers, Jaufre decided to seduce them, with shots of café-calvados, bottled cider, apéritifs. Fair's fair of course! I water you, you feed me with texts. It isn't something which is missed in the office archives and the Town Hall! What harm in it? When Jaufre had studied these papers from way back, he carefully replaces them.'

Doré was terrified. If Mr Figuier came to hear of it, it was instant dismissal.

'On top of that,' continued Lepicq – 'murder! Panic of Doré and Genêtou. The police are going to find the last delivery of documents on Jaufre's table. How they came to be there will have to be explained! That's when they did the briefcase trick; each takes back his property! Neither is seen nor known about!'

'It's true,' Doré admitted. 'We weren't meaning to do harm. Seeing that it had had nothing to do with the crime ... .'

'Unfortunately, I have reasons to believe the contrary!' Lepicq cut in dryly. 'What have you done with the packet of documents?'

'Ah well, I have ... I have since rearranged the items!'

Lepicq felt he was lying.

'Reclassified them!'

'How do you expect me to remember, sir? I couldn't ask for anything better; but it was all in there! A bit of one file, a bit of another. What matter! Come now, sir … . It's not possible that the crime … .'

'Will you announce me to Mr. Figuier,' Lepicq said coldly. 'You'll get the boot, but that will be because you deserve it!'

'Sir, I beg you … . I'm the father of … .'

He was sweating freely; his hands were trembling.

'That's all the same to me. I'm going to announce myself; I've no time to lose!'

Then, under a pile of files, Doré went looking for a folder swollen with sheets of paper.

'Here!' He said. 'I … I … . Excuse me, I still have nothing rearranged. It's all here.'

In his room thirty minutes later, Lepicq stopped short in front of one of these documents. He skimmed through it, then reread it steadily; afterwards he rushed to the window. He examined the paper against the light with the magnifying glass. In turn his own hands were trembling.

* * *

'Scratchings out! Alterations! That's really good. Very careful work! But old Jaufre was found out! He had been imprudent in not keeping his discovery to himself! He had given in to the temptation of thumbing his nose. "You hate me, eh? You despise me, what? Ah well, I'm happy to inform you of what I did, through the greatest of chances, a brainwave! A pleasing brainwave!" And then … they found him dead, on the carpet! Saying that, it's the widow that I have to … .'

It was a day of inspiration. Lepicq was in top form.

'The widow Angat? But it is she who had already offered me the clue, somewhat unknowingly, the other day! When she told me "Saturn and Mars at right angles in House VIII." '

He had raised his face skywards, where astrologers write the zodiacal Houses of the planets – House of Life,

House of Wealth, House of Health, House of Death, House of Visions, House of Enemies … .

'The explanation of the crime? But it was written up there, in black and white! House VIII! Everything came from House VIII!'

★ ★ ★

'Great news, Mr.Lepicq!' Said Mrs. Pibole.

'A new murder?'

'You're going a bit far! No, thank God! Professor Alfa … The well-known seer … .'

She undid a large roll of paper. It was a brightly-coloured poster. Beneath the stylised portrait of the Professor in fur hat, the lawyer read this text:

CRIQUEBEC

Saturday 17 August
At the Business and Sports Café
Soirée at 20.30

TWO HOURS OF MYSTERIES

Following ten years of perilous studies in the Land of Icebergs, the legendary Hypnotist, Magician and Spritualist.

PROFESSOR ALFA

Medium certified by Scientists, Member of the Academy of Occult Sciences. Founder of the Nordic Psychoanalytic Institute,

Will give a gripping Demonstration

OF HIS FANTASTIC POWER
THE MOST FORMIDABLE EXPERIENCES OF THE CENTURY!

THE HYPNOTISING MACHINE. THE DEATH
RAY. MYSTERIES OF THE FAR NORTH. MAGIC
SNOW. MAGNETIC IRRADIATION. THE
MIDNIGHT SUN. PSYCHIC PHENOMENA.
WITCHCRAFT. TELEPATHY. DIVINATION.
PREDICTIONS.

I ANSWER ALL QUESTIONS

I AM INVULNERABLE AND FIREPROOF

*My experiments of Insensibilty disconcerts MEDICAL
SCIENCE. Seeing is believing.
These Experiments will be presented with the aid of men and
women of good will from the audience.*

IN ADDITION !!!
PROFESSOR ALFA
*Will carry out the most formidable experiment which has
ever been attempted*

THE MAGIC MIRROR
ELEMENTAL CINEMATOGRAPHY

*This Experiment will especially fascinate the Town of Criquebec.
By the single force of my will, a dead person will be called up
whose very recent tragic demise is present in all our memories. I will
evoke the re-enactment of this mysterious death. Every one will be
able to follow the unfolding of a terrible scene in my* **MAGIC
MIRROR**, *and recognise*

THE ACTORS

*This sensational experiment will be conducted only on one unique
occasion. I will carry it out in*

THE INTEREST OF TRUTH.

Thus, simultaneously with Lepicq, Professor Alfa had come to a conclusion. Was it the same?

The on-the-spot investigation compared with the method of investigation by correspondence! ... .

Lepicq sat down to eat.

'Blackie! Here, my foolish animal! Here!'

Blackie was the Pibole's dog. A greedy animal, always pushing his muzzle on to one's knees, to beg a scrap of meat, a lump of sugar. The customers said 'Bugger off, scrounger!', accompanying this remark with the toe of their boot.

For that matter, Lepicq usually did not encourage the bad habits of animals. But since he had examined with a magnifying glass the document found in Doré's file, he had formed the habit of summoning Blackie at mealtimes. He patted him, made him lie at his feet and furtively, on the sly, slipped him a large mouthful of all the dishes that the landlady served him, before tasting them himself. When the dog, limpid eyes and tail wild with gratitude, had gobbled up the unappetizing food, licking its chops and demanding more, and it was quite apparent that no harm had been done, then the lawyer in turn stabbed at the plate!

Ever since he had known, he had become like Clémence Maisondieu. He saw poison everywhere!

CHAPTER 13

HOUSE VIII

'Jaufre, is that you?'

The table kicked once.

It was Jaufre.

Outside, a blistering sun, iron-hard.

'Thirty-three in the shade! .... And they were going to see *him* arriving, in an immense bearskin, brow gushing sweat under his fur bonnet!' the people of Criquebec had said, quietly laughing.

Not at all! Professor Alfa, in the flesh, had nothing of an eccentric. Grey flannel suit, lightweight shoes, soft trilby hat; he hardly looked like his poster picture! Average build and rather slim, he looked about forty.

However, he had three things from his poster portrait; a fair jawline beard, unfathomable eyes and a saffron colour. His nimble fingers seemed to be sprinkling liquid about. One felt an electric shock when he shook your hand. Undoubtedly, a considerable seer. The grey flannel suit took nothing away. One imagined perfectly well that dressed as an Eskimo he was impressive. He had brought a suitcase (doubtless his psychic work clothes) and a monumental trunk (materials, apparatus, magic mirror).

He had lunched at the Pibole hotel, where the séance was due to be held in the ballroom. Lepicq watched him below.

The Professor seemed scarcely to have eaten. The people there noticed nothing. When he added salt or pepper, he seemed to proceed with mesmeric passes.

Cutting bread was no longer a routine act, but a magical operation. Drinking became a ritual incantatory procedure. One really felt that this man did not live on earth. He was thinking. Of what? Mystery! Where was his spirit? With the Planets ... . He must be leaping from one zodiacal House into another, running the length of the Arctic and the Antarctic Circles. It was not pleasant when his eye fell on you – he transfixed you. However, you were wrong. Professor Alfa did not see only you! He saw much further ... to the beyond ... . His look plunged to the very depths!

They were many who lunched late this Saturday, for having contemplated Professor Alfa in the process of lunching!

It was now four o'clock.

The old ladies, Lepicq and the Professor were seated around the circular table in the Uranus room. At the Professor's request, the curtains had been only three-quarters drawn. Semi-obscurity bathed the room. In this light, faces and hands took on a spectral appearance. The Professor was right; it was better like this than in complete darkness.

The seer's beard appeared golden.

He had taken over the procedures. Nothing more normal; it was his role. He radiated a tremendous aura. The table had spun immediately, at full gallop. And Jaufre had arrived. It had not taken a lot of persuasion, as on other days. He had to deal with a greater force than himself; with someone who knew how to speak to the dead, and make them listen.

'Jaufre, there is a man in prison that they are accusing of having murdered you. He's innocent, isn't he?'

A single knock – 'Yes'

'You haven't been killed for a matter of money?'

Two knocks – 'No'

In the room dedicated to the planet that aroused mediums and astrologists, the Professor's voice had disquieting resonances. At the ends of the little fingers of their hands, each person was able to feel trembling the little finger of their neighbours.

To accord him honour, the widow had placed the Professor opposite her. He was seated between Zélie and Amandine. After Amandine came Lepicq, Clémence, the widow, Vasseur and Frelasset.

The nervous tension was considerable.

These old ladies almost expected that the dead man, suddenly materialised, manifest, doleful, in the dingy clothes in which they had known him so long, and that horrible wound at the base of the skull and, possibly, a sight of the knife driven inside. Were not the Professor's lips fluorescent? First they all see a pale gleam forming itself, then ectoplasm develops .. . But no. It was only a trick of the light. These phenomena would take place only this evening, in Pibole's ballroom where, for the time being, the Criquebec public was admitted to gaze at the magician's baggage.

Very cool, calm and lucid, Lepicq watched.

For some minutes the servant Noémi had been spying, ear glued to the door. Then, with a wry look accompanied by a short laugh, she had shut herself in the kitchen. 'This seer's a charlatan! Does he have to be foolish for ... .'

Noémi the sceptic had begun to write, in a clumsy hand. That morning she had received a letter containing the 'Chain of Chance':

'Good luck, good health! Continue the chain, make nine copies of it that you will send to nine people to whom you wish good fortune. This chain has had its origin in Flanders. It was an American artillery general who had the idea, and this chain must go three times round the world. Do not break it, bad luck could come. This is not a joke and if you do not send them off as instructed, beware ... .'

So, Noémi the sceptic was laboriously making her nine copies. Because that, that was not superstition! The letter gave some examples:

'*Vilcore House was destroyed within eight days, she had not taken this business seriously. Marie of Roumania sent the copies too late; she was poisoned. Miss Pola Negri owed her luck to having followed instructions … .*'

Zélie also wrote as soon as she was able. It wasn't so much that she believed in luck. But she had no wish to wake up poisoned, like Marie of Roumania … .

'Jaufre,' the Professor spoke, 'you were murdered because you had discovered a secret.'

A secret … . The seer had come to the same conclusion as Prosper Lepicq.

Jaufre's answer:

'Yes.'

'A wicked act was committed earlier.'

'Yes.'

'Someone was frustrated.'

'Yes.'

'Your murderer is really the person whose name has been revealed to me by my astrological calculations?'

'Yes.'

'Jaufre, I will call you this evening. I will return to you your earthly form. You will live again in the magic mirror, as you were on the evening of your death, seated on your bed. The curtains will draw apart, an arm carrying a knife will sweep down; you will die for the second time. We will see your murderer waiting in a corner of the cellar, the murder site, then fleeing through the yard.'

The Professor's voice became even more solemn.

'We will see him fleeing, through the old gate, whose nails caught his clothing and retained the material evidence which will unmask him. Jaufre, you will come?'

'Yes.'

Lepicq scrutinised the faces, fixing in turn the Professor, the widow, Vasseur, Beluge, the Maisondieus, Frelasset … . This latter's teeth were chattering.

The table came down again. The séance was

terminated. With her heavy trot which rattled the floor, Mrs. Angat ran to open the curtains, then clapped her hands:

'Noémi, tea ... .'

Noémi came in, carrying a tray.

Still honouring the Professor, the widow had decided that that day, tea would be served in the Uranus room.

The servant set out the cakes and sugar. The widow filled the cups. Noémi was discreetly regarding the seer with scorn. 'That comedian! ... .' This disdain was so tangible that the widow threw the servant an angry look. Noémi shrugged her shoulders. It wasn't her fault! She couldn't do anything! She was born a sceptic, she would die a sceptic! She wasn't like those rubbernecks on the Square ... .

Mrs. Angat rose and went to the window.

'Look then! All these people ... People know that you're here, Professor!'

The others had joined her and regarded the Square, dark with people.

The widow was gloating. To have under her roof the illustrious Alfa, the foremost medium in the world! A notable honour!

Lepicq returned to the table and took a petit four.

'They will have a crowd this evening at the séance!' he said.

The Professor turned his mesmeric glance towards him but did not reply.

They all took their places again at the round table.

A moment later, as she set down her empty cup, Clémence Maisondieu said to the widow:

'I must congratulate Noémi! She surpassed herself. Excellent, this tea! I put a pinch too much sugar in, but it was perfect, really!'

And her smile abruptly disappeared. She put a hand to her heart while her mouth half-opened, so that her look, wandering from face to face, made her the interrogator,

145

putting they did not know what question – then! Worried, growing distraught, erratic ... . Lepicq, one hand on the back of his chair, as though prepared to jump, looked intensely at Clémence . Her features expressed total incomprehension. The appearance of someone tempted to put their face in both hands and to say 'But look! ... This isn't possible! Not possible! ... I could have deceived myself at that point! She could have guessed? No. *That* isn't going to happen! I don't accept! Me, me, Lepicq, I don't accept!'

All the same, *that* happened.

Clémence stood up suddenly, her chair knocked over, in thrall to a horror which disfigured her and made her put her fingers on her meagre breast. She shouted: 'They have poisoned me ... . Help! ... Help!'

A scene of great confusion followed.

Lepicq raised a fist at the ceiling, without their being able to know who he was getting at. Professor Alfa, suddenly stripped of that aura which made him an almost superhuman creature, was casting anxious looks around and seemed enormously bothered. The old ladies were very dismayed. In the presence of the Professor, letting oneself go like this at the ridiculous imaginings! Letting themselves be caught by childish terrors! This was not really good for Clémence! Especially as Mr. Lepicq had settled everything in finding arsenic in the skins of the stuffed cats!

'Look, my dear friend,' the widow implored. 'A bit of common sense!'

Clémence crumpled. Her mouth contorted. She let out an awful moan, then vomited alarmingly.

An icy pallor spread over the faces of the old ladies. So it wasn't imagination?

Clémence groaned. Her face turned blue. She collapsed. There was no more vomiting.

'Quick! An antidote!' Amandine Maisondieu called out in a strident voice; her face had become dark from emotion. 'I'm running off to Mrs. Gentil's place.'

'I'm going there with you!' Lepicq said.

On the pavement he grabbed Amandine's arm. She freed it with a jerk

'The name of the poison?' He panted.

'For killing flies!' She answered in a broken voice.

Then, she hissed:'I hate you! Oh, how I hate you! ... '.

'What is it, this fly killer?'

'Metallic arsenic.'Then again, hissing:'It's you!' She said. 'It's you who had him killed!'

'You've got a bit of a nerve! But .... Quiet!'

By chance, Dr. Pouacre happened to be at the pharmacy.

He was alarmed.

'Metallic arsenic? It's not possible! I know Miss Clémence; she always imagines ... . I'm quite sure that ... '

'Doctor,' Lepicq cut in harshly, 'I'm quite sure that if someone doesn't intervene immediately, Miss Clémence Maisondieu will dead before this evening! Antidote, quickly! We'll discuss this later!'

'Good good! In this case ... . If you're certain! Iron oxychloride ... . It's more active. Quickly, Mrs. Gentil. Make me a solution of oxychloride at ... .'

He gave the formulation. The pharmacist leapt to her medicine bottles. Feverishly, Dr. Pouacre became involved, placing tiny weights on the precision balance.

He enquired:'Violent vomiting?'

'Very violent.'

'Cocaine then! ... . Fifty milligrams for 500 ml of water, Mrs. Gentil. Quickly ... Quickly ... .'

At the moment he was the more feverish.

He returned to Amandine and took her hands.

'Warm milk, yes? And warm packs. Vigorous rubbing down with tincture of musk. We will pull her out of this, have no fear!'

In the Jupiter room, Clémence Maisondieu was delirious, suffocating and seized with alarming convulsions.

★ ★ ★

'So,' said Lepicq, 'you had worked it out!'

'That this seer had never been a seer in his life?' said Amandine Maisondieu. That he was your own creature? I wasn't deceived for a second!'

The smell of mothballs – the odour of the old Maisondieu residence!

Amandine raised her sullen face.

'You're wondering whether I saw it, your plan! This evening in the ballroom, during this ridiculous séance of conjuring, your poor innocent of a seer would have shown I don't know what magic lantern scene, or they would have seen, following the murdering of Jaufre, a woman made up in such a way to look like me! Since the time that you had realised that it was me who had killed him, you have been obliged to photograph me from all angles, to act as the model to your performer!'

'Wrong! In the seer's luggage there were only stones and scrap iron!'

'Oh?' She said, dumbfounded.

'In any case, the séance at Pibole's would not have taken place! The poster was meant simply to frighten you. The real séance had taken place at the widow's. It's purpose was to persuade you that you were found out, so as to frighten you, to push you into committing some stupidity, giving me proof. ... . Whilst they were calling up Jauffre, I was watching you.'

'So this is why the Professor was against anyone opening the curtains? From prudence!'

'From prudence, absolutely. I thought you were going to be tempted to poison him. Not having seen your pouring out the poison, I went back to the table while you were at the window with the others and, uncertain, I got the table to move one eighth of a turn!'

'So that, if I had poured the poison into Alfa's glass ... .'

' It would have been you who would have drunk it!'

With her old woman's intuition, Amandine had understood that Lepicq was combining his investigations with information that the 'Professor', the seer invented for the situation, was getting from the townsfolk of Criquebec and actively passing on to the lawyer. The man who had solved the riddle of Jaufre's death, the dangerous one, was Lepicq. Also, seeing herself done for, it was on Lepicq that she had decided to get her revenge; she had poured the fly-killer into his cup. So that Lepicq, thinking to save Alfa in making the table turn one place and so bringing the Professor's cup to Amandine, had accidently provoked poisoning of Clémence, by bringing his own cup in this act to the younger Maisondieu's place!

Amandine had placed her hands on her knees. She kept her head directly below the glacial look of the defunct Maisondieus who seemed to be judging her from their lofty frames. 'I wasn't able to do otherwise. I had been pressed. Fate! Fate!'

Fate – a big word, easily let out! And meanwhile ... .

'Was I able to foresee?'

Twenty-four years earlier Adrienne Maisondieu, the mother of the two sisters, had died. The father, Marcellin Maisondieu, followed her three weeks later. Full of years, he had been tyrannised by his daughters. Of the two, it was Amandine who harrassed him more! Spiteful, Marcellin had organised revenge. Or rather, a wicked trick ... . In the will, he left the old family house on the Square to Clémence the younger daughter, and ironically gave to Amandine the house near the church. Amandine discovers the will and chokes with rage. She falsifies the document! It was too easy, scratching out the two christian names and writing the name Amandine where it had been Clémence , and vice versa.

'I was only putting back things into their rightful state! I was the elder! The house on the Square had to come to me. Clémence would have had it on my death.'

'You have been very wrong to give yourself all this trouble! The will was worthless! A father's legacy to children means nothing! In terms of the law, a portion is provided, which only authorises an excess of one quarter.'

'Precisely! I told myself that Clémence would make difficulties, persisting in making use of this will to force me to sell. She would prefer that the house be lost to both of us, rather than ... .'

And it was because of that, because of the haunting memory of this forgery that Amandine passed sleepless nights and every morning woke with a deathly pale face!

'Could I have predicted this?'

Clearly not!

The falsified will had gone through like a letter in the post. Mr. Figuier had hardly read it, since there was no need for provisions of a will for the successions from ancestors to direct descendants! Because the law provided! The document had been preserved only because French usage expected that one preserved the smallest scrap of paper! Archives had not been invented for nothing! And Amandine wasn't able to predict that, twenty-four years later, because that old fool of a Jaufre, interested in graphology, and Genêtou and Doré at the café-calvados, this miserable will would be dug up from the dusty files and end up on Jaufre's table. And Jaufre, interested in graphology could suddenly, and with magnifying-glass, reveal the fraud!

' He came to threaten you?'

'No. A letter. I found it under my door, on returning from the widow Angat's. Jaufre said I have had occasion to study the will of your father. The late Marcellin Maisondieu had a very curious handwriting, very personal ... . Quite interesting! Especially when he wrote your christian name and that of Miss Clémence. It was clear.'

It could not be clearer!

Then, she had slipped on a blue dress; that was enough for her not to be recognised. She had gone out, gripping in her mittened hands the handle of a kitchen knife.

'This letter, you can be sure that Jaufre had not written it for nothing! He was a devil! He wanted to blackmail me! Now, I live modestly, I only hold my position through great thrift! I would not have been able to give him money! Well? He would have triggered off the scandal ... . This disgrace on my name! And Clémence, Clémence who was only awaiting my death to come down here! She would have shouted from every rooftop that for twenty-four years I had stolen *her* house! Perhaps she would have sought to get me evicted, demanded the sale ... .'

All these ideas whirling about in the old girl's head! A blue dress ... . A kitchen knife ... . And go if you please, Mr. Jaufre, to do the graphology in another world!

'It was my house! My house, you understand?' Amandine spoke fiercely.

Lepicq had forgotten that this woman, a moment earlier, had tried to poison him. He was reflecting on the Zodiacal House Number VIII, where sixty-six years previously all these events were already foreshadowed by the presence of some unpleasant planet, by some sinister astral conjunction in Amandine's sky of nativity.

The Eighth House – hadn't he read in a manual borrowed from the widow Angat – *governs the consequences of death: wills, legacies, dowries ...* .

* * *

On the Square the young girls were singing – not loudly because the seer was about – *Am Stram Gram, Femina Godam, Carabim Zigolo.*

After her crime Amandine had not dared to take back the will. But she had stolen the 800 francs and, the following day at dusk, had hidden them in Barnaby's mattress.

At the moment Lepicq's double rôle of detective and

lawyer was simplified. The puzzle resolved, the detective faded back into the shadows. It was now the lawyer who was going to occupy the stage.

Amandine carried around with her a glazed look. She had killed a man and poisoned her sister.

Prison ... .

Ah well, but ... . Prosper Lepicq the lawyer would deliver her from it!

'Dear Miss, we will not despair. You are going to leave me the charge of defending you, matters will be settled better than you think. My defence, I am aware of it, I have it, it is all ready, Miss! Come now! What's at the bottom of all this? The matter of a will?'

Old, very old history! A trifle! Childish!

Amandine, tossing her head with little nods, was approving and quietly smiling.

Lepicq came to the main question. 'Jaufre ... . Jaufre – yes, of course! ... . But Miss, let's not forget what Jaufre was! A dubious character with a troubled past. A master blackmailer! His menacing letter played on your ignorance of the law ... . A moment of panic! Fear of scandal! Legitimate defence, Miss, legitimate defence! Jaufre, I'm putting him in my pocket, and all the Lecorbins in the world will make no difference to it! What remains? Miss Clémence your sister. But I've seen Pouacre. He will save her, he says so. From then on, what? An accident, nothing more! For whom was the poison intended? For me! For me, your support now, but your enemy then! A simple instinct for self-preservation, that too! ... . And the fatality, as you say ... . Let's not throw in our hand. We shall not avoid prison, but we'll be released! If, as there is every reason to hope, your sister escapes, and if, as I really believe, she has no complaint ... .'

'No,' Amandine spoke.

'You are of my opinion, that she will have no complaint?'

152

'That's not what I wanted to say.'

'You're fearful that they won't be able to save her?'

'It's not that either.'

'What then?'

'Prison. I don't want to go to prison.'

'Ah,' said Lepicq scratching the top of his head, 'I follow you very well, but it's ... .'

She took out a sweet box from a drawer, offered a chocolate to Lepicq, took one, as if this day had been a day like the others, that there had been no crime nor poisoning, that it was a matter of a courtesy visit!

As Lepicq's fingers reached his mouth and were about to place the chocolate square between his teeth, the lawyer's expression suddenly hardened. The skin around his cheeks tightened painfully, he suffered a dreadfully cold sensation.

Amandine's look! ... . Terrifying, all sharpened with hate, charged with a keen expectation! Those eyes, earlier glazed and now two embers, revealing a frightening malice, truly devilish.

With horror, Lepicq threw the chocolate away. He gulped with disgust.

'Devil!' she hissed. 'Devil! You know everything!.'

Her breathing had become very short, her hands were clenched firmly on the edge of the table, her nails scratching the wood.

'Poor wretch! What have you done?'

The chocolates were poisoned. Amandine had not hesitated to poison herself, the better to deceive Lepicq, and he had poisoned himself at the same time!

He got up and was preparing to run towards the door, to the chemists.

'No,' she said. 'I don't want to go to prison. I don't want to!'

'Don't you understand that it's better like that? Besides it would be useless ... .'

She sighed.

'God, how I hate you! I would have given everything that you take that sweet ... '

This was monstrous!

She had stopped clinging to the edge of the table; her hands with the fingers curled jumped spasmodically over the wood, like two spiders from a nightmare.

'It was my house! It was my right!'

The suffering was racking her. Burning in her. But she was resisting; she had far more force of character than Clémence.

She leaned forward, made an effort to control the involuntary twitches of her hands – hands which seemed no longer to belong to her, to be two agitated animals with an independent existence. She succeeded. With her right hand she opened the fingers of her left hand and stretched out her palm.

'Look! This life line! Double! Big and red! So long, so long! ... . And these lines across my wrist! Three of them, very deep, and a fourth, very fine – but it's there! One hundred years! ... . A hundred years, you understand? I was made to live for a hundred years!'

She was gasping. Beneath the rush of blood which was rising to her face, her skin was tinged, becoming a brick-red shade, and the whitish patches began to spread; like dying embers of coal.

'A hundred years! ... .'

She broke out into an abominable laugh, savage and tinged with dementia.

'The lines are lying! Like everything else! It's only people and things which lie!'

Silence. Then, in a single breath:

'It's true that the lines cannot predict ... .'

The laughter took her over again:

'Ah well, you will not do it, your speech for the defence, Mr. lawyer! You must look for a client somewhere else!'

She stood up, with some considerable effort. She staggered, held onto the back of a chair, and cast a distressed look around her.

The Maisondieu furniture, the Maisondieu portraits, the drapes, the Maisondieu tablecloths, the floral plates, the Maisondieu knicknacks, the Maisondieu clocks. .... .

The walls were flickering, the furniture was sliding, the whole house was keeling over. She believed the last moment had come and that she was going to die. She threw herself towards that window from where, for so long, she had seen the God-made sun and rain falling on the Square of Criquebec. She wrapped her fingers, so thin that her knuckles cracked, over the window catch. She did not accept dying. She was built for living a hundred years, and she was still only sixty-six. All those years that she should have been able, that she ought to have spent in the Maisondieus house, and that ill-luck had stupidly stolen from her! .... . Then she weakened:

'My God, forgive me! I am only a poor woman who asks little; no more than to live and die in her own house ....'

Ah well, Amandine, is this so terrible after all?

We are definitely going to need to retire your career of the crow of the crossroads who looks out over the chestnut trees. But another Maisondieu, your sister, with a profile just like yours, is going to come and install herself near this crossroads. She in her turn will be the devoted guardian of the Maisondieu relics. She will watch that the linen is not moth-eaten, she will put mothballs in the drawers, and each week she will wind up the clocks (she who cannot abide the noise of a ticking clock!) and they will dutifully beat the seconds, until ... . Until the last representative of the Maisondieus is extinct, the furniture, the drapes, the plates the relics are carried away to the auction sale!

Up above on the plateau, the stone of the family vault will be lifted one last time, then lowered. Here lies Adrienne

Maisondieu, here lies Marcellin Maisondieu, here lies Amandine, here lies Clémence . Here lie all the Maisondieus! Two dates under each name. Pray for them!

And nothing else, in heaven or on earth, will be important!

The pain dragged from her the cry of a child. Suddenly, so that it happens more quickly, so that it is over, she took another chocolate. But her hand missed her mouth; the poisoned chocolate rolled on the floor.

Lepicq was as though paralysed. He had witnessed many tragic scenes, but never a spectacle so unpleasant. He told himself 'I am a murderer! She is dying because of me. What importance has it, that Jaufre's death was not avenged? True, there was Barnaby ... .'

She threw her arms out in front. Made a step. The bed ... . To die on the bed! Not on the floor like a dog. On the bed. It's done like that. It must be done like that. That's how it was always done in the Maisondieu household. Maintaining one's station ... . Dignity ... . 'Jaufre, I will call you this evening. You will appear in the magic mirror'. Ridiculous, this seer! If he imagined that she did not understand ... .

She was delirious

She took another step. Wanted to take it rather; but it did not happen. But it had to! The bed ... The bed ... .

Lepicq supported her.

'I hope they will save Clémence,' she said after a spasm which brought froth to her lips. 'I wished her no harm ... .'

The room was long. The bed was seven or eight steps away from her. A journey ... . An endless journey. The lawyer almost carried the old girl; she threw her arms feebly out in front.

Her fingers were locked, clenched on her palms as they had been clenched on the table. The very sharp fingernails scratched the skin.

Lepicq felt Amandine's breath on his face. She spoke:

'You are content? You are happy now?'

They were approaching the bed; they were almost touching it.

Amandine opened her hands. There was a little blood at the end of the ring finger. She raised her hand in front of her eyes in that familiar gesture that she had made so many times. Surprise overcame her.

'My life line .... Split .... One of my nails has cut it!'

A supreme calm brought peace to her distraught features. Her head drooped to one side. She was still able to murmur, in a strange accent (near religious conviction? Or supreme irony?).

'I was right! The lines do not lie!'

Lepicq lifted the long corpse and carried it as far as the bed. On that bed where so many of the Maisondieus were born and died he laid out old girl, completely in black, on the violet bedspread.

In the rooms the clocks were working for no reason. There was no longer anyone in the house but a stranger.

Lepicq locked the door and left. He went up to the Town Hall and in front of the mayor and the town policeman, made a full report of what he had uncovered, and of the events which had just taken place.

CHAPTER 14

UNDER THE STARS

Professor Alfa removed his gold beard.

'So, my young Jugonde?'

The wizard passed a napkin over his face, making large sections of his saffron-tinted foundation disappear – becoming Jugonde, Prosper Lepicq's secretary.

'You've just passed through a bad moment, Boss?'

'Terrible! I believe I would prefer to confront half a dozen gangsters armed to the teeth rather than one old girl armed only with fly-killer and chocolates!'

Jugonde removed from his eyelids the Khôl powder which was making the eyes unfathomable. His psychic power lay no deeper than the rosiness of his colour, the sparkle of his expression, the brightness of his healthy teeth. His capacity for glamour in the company of the old ladies was wiped away to nothing, but his power of seduction over young girls found itself singularly enhanced.

'The séance on the raising of Jaufre was a bit over the top!'

'It had to be that! You were perfect!' Lepicq said. 'I will not say as much for myself! Hanged if I can imagine at what moment she poured out the poison, right under my nose!'

'Bye the bye – Clémence?'

'The worst is over. The attacks of vomitting were able to make her better. She'll pull through.'

Jugonde now had his normal appearance; a fresh-faced and personable twenty-four year young man.

'Without reproaching you boss, you had entrusted to

me a pretty revolting chore! Interchangeable horoscopes by the dozen! Magical charms by the spadeful! I've had upsetting letters! I positively disgusted myself! Still! The end justifies the means! The seer will have served a good cause!'

'Once is not a habit!' Lepicq threw out sarcastically. Then:

'By the way … . In your recent post, still nothing from Reine Coulemelle?'

'Nothing.'

'Couril was quite right! She made herself a separate world. An existence on the margin. She did it quietly, and finished up by preferring … . She's happy.'

'Happy?'

'Seeing that she turned down Professor Alfa's humanitarian offer.'

'A nutcase!'

'I don't know. Absurd, if you like! So what? Given that they're not numerous, those who live like that, in the secrecy of the heart, a life on the margin!'

Jugonde shrugged his shoulders.

'If that satisfies her … .'

Deep down, it didn't matter to him! He was twenty-four years old, a heart hard to please, warm expression, bold hands … . He smiled, for the benefit of someone who was far from here, in Paris, in the XVIth … .

Lepicq replied. 'The beauty of it is the case of Couril! For him also everything happens inside his head! A dreamer like Reine Coulemelle. The witch's Sabbath, the gallivanting, how farcical! And like everything, becomes easy to explain! The poster dealing with the murderer? What was he risking since he was innocent? But that fashioned him, inflated his character! The anonymous letters? They attributed depraved morals; he goes in for depraved morals! Too happy to seize this opportunity of spicing up his personality! Don Juan! Casanova! Wonderful roles ! "I turn women's heads?" Possible! "I don't take them by force! How

159

the husbands defend themselves!" While probably he had not had a single woman in his life! Women! This constant preoccupation, while he paced eternally up and down, or watched beneath Reine Coulemelle's window! A woman who attended to her toilette, who made herself up, who curled her hair … . A woman! … . He dreamed! And to think that it's he who explained to me the state of mind of Reine Coulemelle! The solitary dwarf was cut out for understanding the solitary postwoman!'

'Confounded little dwarf!' Jugonde burst out, with the indifference of his age.

Lepicq tidied his meagre luggage into his briefcase – shoes, slippers, briefs, pyjamas, Montaigne still in mint condition.

'You're going back to Paris, boss?'

'No! I'm on holiday!'

'Any more need of me?'

'Not at all, my young Jugonde. Finished! Sorted!'

'Then … .'

Jugonde held out his hand. He went down the stairs four at a time, running to catch the old banger which would drive him to the station. He was in a hurry to get back to Paris, because of a young girl who lived in the XVIth … .

In turn Lepicq went down, quietly. He paid his bill and handed over two envelopes to the bellboy, with a forty sous tip.

'Take these to the postman for me!'

One of these envelopes was intended for Médéric Plainchant. It contained a visiting card on which the lawyer had simply written this number: 14. Fourteen, in the brochure of the Language of Flowers, corresponded to Balm which signified *Have more audacity!*

The other envelope was for Zélie. Lepicq had written on her card 178. It was the number for the button rose, which signified *You will marry shortly. All my good wishes!*

And he took himself off. He went to Havre on foot, as he had planned on leaving Paris. He left Criquebec without drum nor trumpet, without taking leave of these old women, without bothering to know whether the widow Angat had taken her erection of the sky of nativity to a satisfactory conclusion.

He went at a good pace. He was nimble and lively. He had not made a sou from the Jaufre affair but all the same he was content. The route upon which he advanced was a good one. He felt himself active and smart as a devil. The sun was still beating down agreeably, but with moderation. Its rays were not beneficial for deep and obscure reasons, They were beneficial because they were warm, neither more nor less.

An end to superstitious omens! A bootlace which unties itself anounces neither good nor bad news. It says it must be retied! A magpie flies off to the left; a sign for worry? Absolutely not! … . It's a sign that it's wanting to fly off! A crow flies away to the right; a sign of misfortune? Well no! It's a sign it heard the noise of my footstep. It's a prudent fellow, he shoots off! Good trip Mr. Crow!

Lepicq dined in a small, unnamed village, and it went off very well.

He set off with a spring in his step. He had eaten with a good appetite; his stomach had no creases!

He was so content that he decided not to sleep in a hotel that night. He slept in the open, under a haystack, under the stars.

Stretched out on his back, head wedged on his briefcase, he contemplated for a moment the Milky Way, the Great Bear, the Pole star, and other components of the celestial clock. Blue on the horizon, Venus was giving him the eye.

'I am Venus; I am the most beautiful! I command the throat and the chin; I produce musicians, painters, hairdressers, artists of every sort!'

161

In the void of the night, the spheres turned.

Lepicq was hearing voices:

' I am Saturn. It's not for nothing they call me the Great Misfortune! I am addled with wickedness! Distrust, Lepicq!'

'This pretention!' another voice replied. 'Who holds the levers of command for a quarter of an hour? It's I, Jupiter, otherwise called the Great Fortune! I am an old man and I wish this small-town lawyer well!'

'I am Neptune the mystery planet,' said Neptune. 'I provide intuition and even second sight. I wish no harm to this Lepicq, but I am currently in exile in House XII; what do you want me to do?'

'I am Mercury, I act on the cerebellum and the toes,' Mercury spoke, with the accent and glibness of a sales representative. Nine times out of ten my subjects are little smart-arses! My elemental radiations are top quality and my vibratory tone without equal! Ask for the trademark Mercury! ... .'

'I am the Moon,' said the Moon. 'They know me; there's nothing more to do about my reputation. I command the right eye in men and the left eye in women ... .'

In this way, in the sky of Lower Normandy, on the thresholds of their zodiacal houses, the planets gave their sales patter, like street vendors!

Already half asleep, Lepicq stirred good-humouredly.

'But not so!' he muttered. 'All this is a joke! And for a start ... there are no planets!'

THE END

POSTSCRIPT

'The Old Ladies' Tea Party' was edited in 1937 by Gallimard, after having been prepublished in serial form in 'Regards' if one believes Thierry Picquet.

Curiously, it was re-edited only very belatedly, in 1984, then in 1991, when it was a matter of one of the more successful investigations of Prosper Lepicq, and in many respects the most surprising... .

In his study 'Pierre Véry or the police in fairyland'[1] Francis Lacassin has analysed the sources of Véry's inspiration very well and noted the importance of everything in the mystery novels which is concerned with the strange and the fantastic. He has highlighted what the poetic Véry owes to what he calls with pleasure 'wonderful rhetoric'. "The 'wonderful rhetoric' is represented in his work by the nursery rhymes, prophecies, horoscopes, letters of good fortune, novelty verse, popular songs, promotional slogans, nicknames, and names of forebears. Sentences or ends of sentences, Pierre Véry phrased his fairy tales for grown ups with the same application as Tom Thumb scattering his pebbles."

It is perhaps in 'The Old Ladies' Tea Party' that this wonderful rhetoric is exercised with the most brilliance, with the most consistency. Here, examples are plentiful, from the bizarre nursery rhyme declaimed by the young girls playing tag on the Square, to the horoscopes and wild publicity of the strange Professor Alfa, the unlikely founder of the Nordic institute of psychoanalysis,

---

1. 'Pierre Véry or the police in fairyland'. In *Mythology of the police novel*, volume 2 by Francis Lacassin, collection 10/18, no. 868, 1974.

and passing through the false coded message of Jaufre, and the signs on the Criquebec shops: 'For the Good Swordsman', 'At the Wish to Please', 'For the Wasp-Waisted.'

On top of this wonderful rhetoric there is added a sort of everyday wonder like the description of Miss Zélie Beluge's shop window, where toys are placed side by side, comics, papers decorated with 'wishes at the end of the year and sentimental declarations', jokes and tricks (the list is a poem in itself: snowstorm tablets, shivery rosettes, sparkling handshake, devil's log, volatile paper ...), defecators, this evidence of good French taste, that lavatorial item long since fallen into desuetude but which amused the generations.

Lastly, a third sort of magic is there in abundance in the work, that which Francis Lacassin calls 'social wonderment', which is expressed in the different methods of supernatural forecasting employed by the women of the family circle (the numbered stars passing through dreams, the cards, the palmistry ...), in the 'flower language' which serves as code in the silent conversations of Médéric Plainchant and Zélie Beluge, in the cures of the old ducks and the safeguards with which the absent old ladies swap recipes.

All these levels of wonderment endow the town of Criquebec with a definite fairylike quality. However, Prosper Lepicq has been led there by a team of butterflies, as in earlier fairy tales. There is a good deal more. 'Fairyland also admits to an increase in the number of strange people', Francis Lacassin tells us. Criquebec does not miss out on them – Couril the dwarf who always paces up and down, and blames himself anonymously for the worst depravities, Barnaby the mute prattling like a magpie, Reine Coulemelle the postwoman who gives herself over each evening to a very strange ritual in front of the mirror. And others still more ... .

But beneath this fairyland scene there is a real world, trivial and banal. The 'wonderful' is only there because it is drawn out and developed by Pierre Véry's observations.. He does not so much minimise the rest, the greyness of life, the day-to-day emotions which exercise the residents of Criquebec and regulate their relationships (matters of self-interest and inheritance, unfaithfulness, aversion to differences ...). And it is in the real world that crimes *happen, that Jaufre is murdered for a motive very worldly and human. 'The Old Ladies' Tea Party', beneath its shiny exterior, gives an extraordinary picture of a prewar town and its residents, a precise and astute description of a particular French province that the author knew well … .*

The reader notes that Prosper Lepicq resolves the little puzzles of the fairy tale as well as that of the identity of Jaufre's murderer. And that in the resolution of the latter he deploys the whole arsenal of the detective : producing the trap which leads the murderer to being revealed, provoking confidences of the townsfolk, invading privacy to tap minds.

Finally we note that 'The Old Ladies' Tea Party' contains some information on the previous history of the lawyer-detective. 'Lepicq mentioned certain criminal affairs of which he had found the solution before the police. The abduction of the priest Bertrant. The visions of Miss Dorothée F. Bridge. And the affair of the Phantom speaker which had got the whole of France laughing.'

A similar type of case was solved by Sherlock Holmes, mentioned but not recorded by Watson in the work of Sherlock Holmes. The celebrated 'untold stories' have provoked vague apocryphal tales … . But who could have caused Prosper Lepicq to be revived?